A SUNCASTLE UNIVERSE SHORT STORY

THE ONE SHE NEEDS

MARISSA J. GRAMOLL

PRAISE FOR MARISSA J. GRAMOLL

"A Game Like Ours deserves alllllll the stars. I couldn't put it down!"

— BOOKISH HEIDI

"Marissa brought to life such a deep, emotional, and well written story that hooks the reader from the very first page."

— KYRE DAVIDSON

"This author is one of the best in the LGBTQ+ genre."

— M. JAE COOPER

CONTENT WARNING

The One She Needs is recommended for mature audiences.

As an author of emotionally deep works of writing, I don't shy away
from difficult topics. This short story contains violence between two
friends. It also contains references to abusive relatives of one of the
main characters.

PLAYLIST

"Love In The Dark" by Adele
"Yesterday" by The Beatles
"Fast Car" by Tracy Chapman
"Jolene" by Dolly Parton
"Love Me Wrong" by Allie X, Troye Sivan
"I Won't Give Up" by Jason Mraz
"Chasing Cars" by Snow Patrol
"In Your Eyes" by Peter Gabriel
"Breathe Me" by Sia
"Let Her Go" by Passenger
"The Night We Met" by Lord Huron
"Hard To Love" by Lee Brice
"In The Light" by The Lumineers
"All For You" by Sister Hazel

For everyone who wants to share their stories.

Keep going.

The world needs your voice.

WILLARDSON HIGH
SENIOR YEAR
MAY 2009

Bobby

If I could change the past, I would. Can't stop thinking about her.

English gets out. My eyes scan the dozens of Willardson High kids crammed in the hallway. Can't see Lexie anywhere.

You shouldn't be looking for her in the first place, Bobby.

I grind my teeth together wondering when I'll let this go. Been trying for months. My own damn fault for never even flirting with Lex before she and Cody got together. This isn't just the *love who you can't have* situation, either. I was super close to asking her out.

A mix of bad timing and other painful factors.

High school fucking sucks. It sucks for me, and I have it better than most. Can't imagine how bad it is for everyone else.

It isn't right for me to want my best friend's girl. I know it's not. There's not any part of it that's ethically reasonable.

Then again, most of us aren't ethically reasonable. It's high school.

The class before lunch is the only period we don't all share. Lexie looked a little sad this morning in homeroom. I wanna make sure she's doing alright.

That's his job, not yours. I look at my best friend, Cody Jones. A hair taller than me. Blond and charismatic. One of the most popular kids in school, against all odds. Mostly for his epic skill at pitching baseball. Usually the poor kid living in a dumpy trailer, wearing the same dirty old clothes, *isn't* the one who's popular. But well, Willardson High isn't quite the typical place. Not that I'm judging him. If it'd fly with everybody, he'd just sleep at my house instead of that shitty place he lives.

"Hey, Bobby," Vanessa says all smooth, with a wink.

"Hey, V." I give her a hug. "Good to see ya."

"I've gotta run. Call me later, k?" She blows a kiss with two of her fingers.

"K." I wave as she rushes through everybody.

"Cody, Bobby!" Walking the halls, we get fistbumps and high fives.

The popularity is nice. One less thing to worry about. He can pitch and I can hit. Baseball's bigger than football at this school. The whole town worships us. The stands fill up at every game.

"How you doin', Bobby?" Anna brushes my shoulder with her hand, peeking under the fabric of my polo to tickle my deltoid.

"I'm good, Anna. How you doin'?" I lean toward her.

"Could be better," she bites her lip, running her finger up and down my skin. "Maybe we can get together soon?"

"You got it," I promise.

"Can't wait." She walks backward a few feet, waving goodbye.

"You're gonna make me sick." Cody bumps my shoulder.

"Why? You jealous?" I bump him back.

"Yeah right. I've got it all." He flashes a smug smile. Absolutely right. I'd trade everyone else who flirts with me for a chance with Lexie. It's not even a question.

Our lunchroom buzzes with loud chatter. I put a salad on my tray and reach for a skim milk. Two days until our next baseball game. Light meals today. Carb load tomorrow. Stick to the plan. Stick to the meal schedule. Play at my best.

"You see Lex?" I yell to Cody so he can hear.

"No, why?" It's clear he doesn't have a clue.

"Didn't she look sad this mornin'?" I grip my tray, wondering why he didn't notice. She was practically crying when she walked into homeroom. Her eyes all puffy. Didn't say a word all of class. Isn't like her to be anything but bubbly.

"She didn't mention anything." He pulls his fossil of a phone out of his pocket, the flip screen cracked in three places. "Yeah, she hasn't said a word." His thumbs run over the buttons–he has to click each several times to get to type the right letters–to send her a short love note.

It should be me.

I swallow hard. This isn't gonna help. I've got attention from so many girls in this school. Just not the one that matters.

"Can you believe Rutherford? I mean, why do we already have another paper? We just finished that other assignment. Ugh. I was up 'til three am working on last night." Cody grabs a chocolate milk and puts it on his tray while we wait in this forever long line. "Aren't they supposed to go easy on us senior year? I mean we've done our time."

"Easy? Mrs. Rutherford doesn't know that word." I glance at his tray. "Just the milk?"

"I already ate."

"You liar." I scoot my plate over and grab a salad for him. Two bananas. Two rolls. Then I put one back. I don't need extra carbs until tomorrow.

"One day, when I'm playing MLB ball and living in the mansion next to yours, I'm gonna pay for school lunch for all your kids, for their entire high school career. Just to make up for all these little favors you do for me." There he goes again, droning on about how he'll pay me back someday.

"I've told ya ten times. Mom loads up my account. I don't even come close to running out." I nod at a few buddies while we walk to our table. "Let me buy ya lunch once in a while."

"Nope, this is just a loan. I'll pay it all back and then some." Cody raises his eyebrows for emphasis.

"Jesus, that took you guys long enough," Mickey greets us as I set down my tray. "You better eat quick. Lunch is already half over."

"I think everyone was runnin' late today." Trish sets her purse on the side of the chair and sits across from Mickey.

"Never thought English was gonna get out. Then we got caught by a million people in the hallway." I put my backpack under my chair and stretch out my arms. They've been giving me a fit after sitting still all morning.

"I'm still feeling yesterday's game too." Cody grabs my arm, pulling it into a better stretch.

"Glad we get a day between." I return the favor.

"Where is–" Cody's eyes dance around the lunchroom, finally worried about Lex.

And there she is.

Beautiful.

Brilliant.

Bobby's?

I wish.

"Your girlfriend?" Lexie sneaks up behind Cody, raising up on her tippie toes to cover his eyes like a blindfold. She looks a million times better than she did earlier. I stop worrying.

"Yes, you. Hey, babe." He sets his tray on the table and spins around to give her a kiss. My mind wanders to what it would feel like if I was the one kissing her. The one being kissed.

My chest warms with want. Freaking hormones spike up my cock. No, no, *no*. Not now. Not about her.

"Bobby and I were looking all around for you, babe." Cody wraps his hands around her ass, pulling her closer to him.

"Art got out late." She's definitely a lot happier now. Happy with *him*.

Shit. I sink into my seat and force down some bites of food, willing my boner to relax. Why am I so into her? It's just getting worse. Seeing the girl I've had a crush on for ages dating my best friend.

I had no clue he was gonna go out with her. Bastard.

What did I expect? That he'd ask for permission when I've never even told him how I feel about her? Obviously not.

All I want is to be with her. To take her out. Too late now.

My cock perks up like it wants to be closer to her. Jeez. I readjust my tight jeans. Need to rub one out before next period or I'm gonna be hurting sitting in my seat behind her through fifty minutes of history.

I'm lost without her all the time.

Need a distraction. Now.

Pulling out my Motorola Droid, I text my favorite Enby, Sam. Wish they were here. Too bad they live an hour away. Wildcats baseball has next Saturday off since we're about to have playoffs. My folks won't care if I drive to see Sam as long as my homework's done.

Me: Can I come see you next weekend?

Sam: I'd love that!

Maybe I'll take them off somewhere fun. Sure do miss them. We could make out in the back of a movie if it's dark enough. Sam's such a good kisser, too. There we go. Much better to fantasize about someone I'm free to be with.

No one here knows I'm bi, not even my best friends. That's why I'm super careful what I text. They don't have a clue Sam is *more* than a friend to me. A fuck buddy with a luscious cock. That's what they are.

Cody knows I've been with guys before, hell he may even think I'm gay. But I've never been just gay, I'm bi. Always have been, I guess. If being gay is so taboo in our hometown, then I don't wanna know what awkwardness would come out of the closet with me.

So yeah, Cody sorta gets it. We don't really talk about it much. Don't have to. It doesn't really matter. Not to him anyways.

Hate that with so many others it *does* matter. Part of why Cody's my best friend is because he doesn't treat me any different. I can be real with him when I'm fake to everyone else.

Maybe one day I can be real with Lex?

"Did you work on anything fun today?" Cody slouches in the chair next to mine, eyes on this angel in front of us. He casually jots some things in his cheap notebook that he uses as a journal, looking up at Lex every few seconds. Maybe he's writing about her.

Lexie's wearing a lacy white dress and a cute denim vest that got some paint splattered from art class over the right pocket. Her bright red curls cascade beneath a Von Dutch trucker hat. There's a little paint in her hair too.

So freaking cute.

Trish's look coordinates, of course. She's in the reverse outfit of Lex. A tight denim dress with a white lacy vest. Boho headband instead of a hat. They're always wearing matchy stuff. Makes all the other girls jealous of the things they wear and the friendship they have. I'm not totally sure how, but they ended up the big trend setters at Willardson. Next week ten girls will be wearing some copycat of today's ensemble.

"I'm doing a compliment to the blue butterfly." Lexie's smile shines against the fluorescent lights.

"The blue butterfly? Which one is that?" Cody folds up his notebook and tucks it in his old backpack. I wanna punch him.

Which one is that? It's only Lexie's signature piece that she worked on for months.

When I saw it the first time, my eyes got wet because it was like her soul spoke through the canvas. And I'm not a sappy art fanatic by any means. But that painting made me feel so much.

"If you woulda been at the senior exhibit, you woulda seen it." I nudge Cody. "It's her best work yet." My heart beats faster, remembering that as one of the best nights I've ever had. He missed the whole damn thing. But man, she was amazing. Soaking in all the praise like she didn't deserve it. Oh how she did, though. She deserved every bit of praise and then some.

"Here's a pic." Lexie pulls up photos on her brand new iPhone.

"Ohhhh, you've shown me that one. I'll remember for next time." Cody winks at her. Is he even a good boyfriend? Like really? Because he stands her up all the time and apparently can't keep her paintings in his head. I could pick out a Lexie Hawthorne Original from a wall of art, any day. They're absolutely memorable. He's being a dork. Can't even see what he has in front of him.

Or maybe I'm just obsessed with her?

I could talk about her paintings for hours. Every one she's done over the last four years. Cannot wait to see what she does later in life.

I need to stop.

Just like I control the carbs, I need to control my thoughts about Lexie. I'd be such a good boyfriend though. Show her the world she's been missing with Cody's sorry attempts of dating.

"Mrs. Rutherford told me that if I don't get an eighty-five on that paper then I'm not gonna pass her class." Mickey takes a bite of his PB&J.

"Eighty-five? That's doable." I sip the skim milk. It's gross, even though I've been trying to get used to the lack of flavor.

Put calories where they count. Mom always says.

I steal a sip of Cody's chocolate milk. Just one sip won't matter.

Much better.

"Yeah right." Mickey shakes his head. "The highest she's ever given me on a paper is a sixty-nine."

"You wish you got more sixty-nines." Trish pokes her fork in his direction. "Whatever happened to you and Mary Beth?"

Mickey stares at Trish for a minute. "Ask her." He tries to play it cool but I can tell he's mad about whatever it is that went down.

I give Mickey a sad smile. My parents spend hours with me to make sure I get good grades. He doesn't have anyone at home who gives a shit. Dating Mary Beth seemed to help all that. Guess she's out of the picture.

"Did you try talking to the tutors at the library?" Trish offers.

"They wanted eight bucks an hour." Mickey slaps the table, his short temper about to go off. School's always been a really touchy subject for him.

"Let me read it before you turn it in. I know how Mrs. Rutherford operates." I take a bite.

"You have her wrapped around your finger like every female in this school, don't you?" Trish takes a bite of her apple.

"Nah," I take a bite, "she doesn't like anyone."

"Bobby!" Benny tossels my hair. "Who you taking to Prom?"

"Hey," I smooth out the mess he made of my style. "Boundaries, Benny, boundaries."

"I mean it. Who you goin' with?" Benny sips from his orange juice.

"Trish, what's the plan?" I watch her grab her planner out of her bag.

"We haven't talked about it yet." She flips to the page with tomorrow's date on it.

"You guys sure wait 'til the last minute." Benny nods at Nathan who's waving at him from across the lunchroom. "Catch y'all later," he navigates through the tables.

"Lexie love," Trish motions for her to come over to the chair next to her. Lexie's curls bounce as she plops next to Trish. I imagine her plopping that way on my lap. Wrapping my arms around her. My lips on that cute spot of skin right below her earlobe. Whispering sweet words. Asking her how her morning was. Making her night.

Ouch, I pull at my zipper. I need her something fierce.

Not. An. Option.

"You drinkin' my milk again?" Cody's sitting by me, pulling the extra salad off my tray. "Mickey? He's drinkin' my milk again ain't he?"

"Here, lemme give you some more." I go to pour skim milk into his open carton.

"Get that witch's piss away from me." He swipes the milk far away while I grab at it.

"Boys, boys!" Trish snaps her fingers. "This is important!" She waits until we quit horsing around and shows us her planner.

"We can all go to Outback Steakhouse on Fifth Avenue. Or Lexie says the country club for dinner."

"Nope, nope, nope." Cody shakes his head, sporting a ridiculous chocolate milk mustache. "I'm gonna pick up my girl and we'll meet you all there," he reaches across the table for her hand. Soft fingers with french manicured nails grasp his calloused palm.

"That's what you want, ain't it babe?" He holds her eyes and it's like time stops. I wish so much to be looked at that way. To have more than the bathroom jerk offs and a handful of one night stands.

To have her in my arms.

Wait, what? They aren't coming with us? We aren't all going to prom together?

"Alright, whatever. But you have to promise me we're all gonna dance together. Live out senior year with a bang." Trish says.

"Promise." Cody nods.

"Okay, so do you guys wanna meet up?" Trish looks at me and Mickey.

"I'm not sure I'm goin'." Mickey looks at his hands. "Because apparently I need to sell my soul to the devil to pass Rutherford's class. But I'll swing by for a bit if I can."

Guess prom's gonna tank. If we aren't all going together, what's the point?

"Well if y'all don't wanna make plans I'll just do something with Jimmy." Trish pops a piece of bubblegum in her mouth.

"Yeah, you will." Jimmy leans down and kisses her cheek. "Hey, beautiful."

"Pop a squat." She tilts her head to the chair next to her.

"I get the coveted table today, huh?" Jimmy sets down his tray.

"It's not that coveted. I've told you a dozen times we can eat together." Trish plants a kiss on his lips.

"It *is* that coveted." Jimmy's got a big slice of pizza that looks so full of greasy goodness. I stare at my empty plate. Already finished my salad. My stomach grumbles as I toss the roll onto Cody's plate before I eat it.

"Thanks," Cody mumbles with his mouth full.

"I can't wait for you to see my dress." Lexie shimmies her shoulders. "Trish and I spent hours looking for it."

"I'm so excited to pick you up. Thanks for letting it just be us."

Cody reaches for her hand again. He rubs his fingers up and down her knuckles. "It's gonna be the best. I know it is." He's got all this confidence, but a weird feeling takes over my throat.

What if he doesn't show? What if he tells her all this today and tomorrow, it doesn't even matter?

I look at her gorgeous green eyes, wondering if she's really happy with him. Wondering if she'd be happier with me?

I shouldn't think these things. She's his. Not mine. Never will be.

I've got Sam and a dozen girls at Willardson. Probably should've asked one of them to prom. Little late now. Thought we were all going as friends.

We gather up our backpacks and take care of our trays. Heading toward history, I stagger behind with just Cody.

"You better make it." I grip his shoulder, halting him out of earshot. "You've missed so many important moments. She needs you to be there for this one."

"Of course." He agrees, shaking his head. "The other times I didn't mean to…"

"I know, I know." I wrap one arm around him and walk down the hall. "But this is prom. She needs you to whisk her away like Cinderella."

"Pumpkin carriage is at the ready," he smiles. "Guess that makes *you* Fairy Godmother, then."

"You wish I had that kind of magic." I chuckle.

"I know you have that kind of magic." He snickers. "Gonna start calling you Fairy Godmother all the time."

"And who are you? Prince Charming?" I roll my eyes. "Let me know if you need me to pick you up and drive you to her place."

"Thanks. I will," his confidence lets me dare to hope he means it this time.

"You saw how sad she was this morning. Make sure she's doin' alright."

"You think about everything, don't ya?" There's a bit of rudeness in his tone. For a second, I panic. Has he figured it out? I mean he's smart as fuck. But I really do try not to act any different.

That's stupid. He doesn't know I have a crush on her.

"I overthink everything. Duh." I stare into his blue eyes hoping he's hearing this. "She needs you to be a good boyfriend."

"Or what?" Cody's defensive tone makes me on edge. What if he does know? Then he's an ass for never giving a shit. It's not like that. It can't be. I won't believe he has any clue or that would mean him being with her started out all wrong.

"There is no *or what*. You're with her. Be the one she needs."

The bell rings. I open up the door and watch him sit next to Lexie in history. I take the seat behind hers and gear myself up to endure the torture of being behind all that I can't have.

* * *

AFTER BASEBALL PRACTICE, I SPEND WAY TOO LONG WORKING ON MRS. Rutherford's paper. My parents are both working late. The house is so quiet. We need to get a cat or something. It's too lonely here now that Cody only hangs out with Lex. I miss him. Miss all the times we used to do homework together and then play hours of Diablo.

I read over the chapter, skimming for what may help with the paper. The words start blurring together. Feels like my brain is about to explode.

My phone buzzes with a text.

Vanessa: Thinking about you…

I stare at my notes figuring that an hour or two with Vanessa sounds like just what I need. Dialing her number, I hear her answer after the first ring.

"Hey, sugar. You wanna meet up?" There's no mistaking the intent in her voice. Vanessa and I have been hooking up on and off since we got back from winter break. She has a fall birthday too, so we're both eighteen. One of my favorite people to hook up with.

"You and Andy broke up?" I like to make sure. No way am I gonna do anything if she's taken.

"And I need you to cleanse my palate." She's used this line before. It's cute. I'm the go to guy for a good night and no drama. Just sex.

"My place or yours?" I close my text book, so ready for this escape.

"My folks won't be home for a while. Come on over. Give me half an hour?"

"See you then." I click off the phone, shave, shower and head to her place with a handful of condoms in my jean pockets.

She lives a block away. The weather's nice so I walk. Good to get moving after just sitting on my butt for hours. Calories won't shed themselves.

I knock a few times, looking at the flowers dying in the pot on their porch.

"Hey," Vanessa opens the door. Her long black hair is in a heap of curls on top of her head. Bright blue eyeshadow coats her dark eyelids. She's wearing a braless white tank top, nipples poking out of the thin fabric. Her turquoise beaded necklace catches my eye.

"Come on in," she leads me into her house, up the stairs to her room. Leggings hug her gorgeous booty. I lick my lips. This is a great idea.

"What happened with Andy anyway?" I set my backpack on her floor and kick off my shoes.

"I think we were all wrong for each other." She locks her door and brings me to her bed. "And when are you gonna get into a relationship, hm?"

"Me? Never." I chuckle but then it hits me. That sting in my throat grows like every other time I think about Lexie. Think about how there's no one else I'd try to go steady with.

"Never? Yeah, right. There's someone. What's her name?" Vanessa seems to find it funny how awkward I feel at this question.

"Nah, there's no one."

Lexie's my secret. No one knows how I feel.

"I've known you long enough to know there's someone." Vanessa looks thoughtful. "Tell you what." She straddles my lap, working at the top buttons of my shirt and pulling it off of me.

"Whatever her name is, you can think about it," she brings a kiss to my lips. I ease into her warm, lush taste.

"While you kiss me tonight," she takes my hands and brings them under her tank top to the soft skin of her chest. "And touch me." She pushes on my shoulders until I'm laying on her pillows. "Let me be her tonight. Whoever she is." She unlatches my belt. Unzips my jeans. Frees my dick from all clothing.

Something about it makes me feel guilty. I shouldn't be thinking about Lexie while I'm with Vanessa. It's....not right. But she says it's okay. Doesn't hurt to try, right? No one has to know.

"And let me be whoever you want me to be." I lift up her shirt, imagining Lexie here. It's almost like I can see her straddling me, making me as hard as I've ever been.

"Oh, I will." Vanessa leans into my touch. I rub her nipples, grab handfuls of her scrumptious boobs.

It's Lexie's chest. Her body responding to mine.

"See, I knew that would turn you right on." Vanessa eyes my cock, throbbing and *excited* about my fantasy.

"Guess you're right." I smile. We're doing this. I can see she's into it, so I let go of my worries and pretend away.

"You love the role plays." She winks. "And I love when you're so eager." She licks her top lip. "Not that you're ever lacking. But when you're really into it, it's fuckin' fireworks." She slips off of her leggings. I grab the condoms out of my pocket before my jeans fall from my ankles.

"I'm glad you wanted me to come over." I finger her clit, closing my eyes, inhaling her scent as if it's Lexie's. The way she'd feel under my fingertips. The way she'd moan.

Vanessa strokes my cock. I bite open a condom. She rubs some lube along her entry. "Give me everything you wanna give her." She descends upon my cock. I take a deep breath, my head arcing against the pillows. *Oh, Lex, I've always wanted to do this with you.* We work into a rhythm, my hands pulling her hips up and down.

"Ohhhh, ohhhh, ooooooo." It's not Vanessa. It's Lexie. She's my angel. I'm filling her with the best time of her life.

"Fuck yes," I'm in another dimension. The one where I get to be with her. She's all I need. I'm the one who holds her. Kisses her. Touches her.

We rock back and forth. Mine, I just want her to be mine. I think of her red curls in my fingers. Think about how much I'd make her squirt all over me. How there's nothing I wouldn't do for her.

She slips off me and positions on the edge of the bed. I stand behind her, tapping deep into her G-spot. She's screaming my name. I grip her boobs that fill my hands and then some. Pinch her nipples. She bounces against the mattress while I level her into orgasm after orgasm until I climax with her at the end.

We collapse, exhausted as fuck. That was transcendental. I swear I've never come that hard. Hot damn. I hold her close, a layer of sweat sticking us together.

"Thank you." I kiss her neck, getting up to clean us off.

"Okay, whoever this mystery girl of yours is, she's gonna be one lucky girl." She flips over, handing me a tissue. "Because fuck Bobby, you're always good. But that was out of this world."

If I ever get to be with Lexie, it will be even more.

"**Y**esterday" by The Beatles plays in my head like a wish of a better time.

This ain't better. Nope, nope, nope. Am I in for it now....
I'm about to miss prom and stand up my date.

The weight on my chest gets heavier the later it gets. I'd do anything to be there. Nothing will help. Nothing will change. Nothing will fix my mistakes.

You better make it. Bobby's words echo in my head. He's always telling me how to not screw things up.

If only I could've listened this time.

So many problems compounded, leading me to this moment–the biggest of which is our power bill, overdue. Mama's paychecks cover rent. My paychecks *usually* cover utilities. The check to Willardson Electric bounced. Because of Kevin.

Some father you are. Nothing more than a sperm donor.

It isn't like I have a choice. Even if we had the money, I'd be here. Uncle Denver will pay me enough to barter with Willardson Electric, I hope. Gotta keep the lights on, give my sisters and brother some sense of security in their own home. I try so hard to give them a little bit of stability.

Lexie needs stability too.

Gosh darnit. Life pulls me in a million directions. I can't figure out which way to go.

Really wish I could journal my thoughts and get them outta my head. Writing is my salvation. The only way I cope with all the stress.

I've been working as hard as I can, as much as four grown men combined. Not too bad for an almost eighteen year old, but I'm barely keeping up.

Actually, I'm drowning in work–scrap metal piles high. I'm lugging heavy stuff around. Gotta keep my head above water.

I have to get to Lexie *and* I have to get the money from working. Life would be so much easier if I only had to worry about one.

Denver's cutting costs and that means I'm picking up all the labor. I wish Kevin was around. We haven't seen him in a few months. I know he's still alive, living it up somewhere far away from us, because the bank called last week to tell me my account's overdrawn. Again. Who needs family? He has booze. But I could use a hand...even his.

Nope, that's not true either. It's better without him. I'll gladly watch him syphon money from my account if it means he'll stay away a little longer. Even when he's dipping into my funds, stealing my hard earned wages, I'd rather have that than have him at home.

My back burns. Thinking about Kevin ignites the pain like it just happened, even though I haven't seen him in a while. Trauma lives in the muscles and bones, I swear.

Bobby was there for me right after Kevin screwed me up. I've never thanked him for that. He wanted to know why I was beaten black and blue, but I couldn't handle him knowing. Wouldn't do any good for him to hear my sob story. All I did was write down my thoughts in a crappy cheap notebook and bury it somewhere no one will ever find.

Kevin's old man hit him and so did my great granddaddy before that. Like trauma lives in muscles and bones, abuse runs in families. All I can do is break the cycle.

You better make it. Bobby's always right about stuff like this. Heck, he's always right about everything.

Unlike me. The loser. Today, yesterday, *forever?*

Hauling another load from one side of the junkyard to the other, I look over my shoulder to see if Denver's watching from his throne on the tow truck. Nope. I think he went to take a piss so I have a sec to text my girl. She's gotta be worried sick by now.

I wipe the grime off my fingers and pull my phone from my pocket. The phone ain't responding. Dang thing. This battery is on its last leg, doesn't work more than a few hours, and I've been here way longer than that. Started at this dump right after I walked my sisters to school first thing this morning.

Swatting my phone doesn't resurrect it. *Come on, come on, come onnnnnnn.* I press all the buttons, hoping for even just a little bit of juice. Nope, not today. I grind my teeth hard together knowing I'm gonna be in the doghouse over this one. Or worse.

She could break up with me.

A shiver works through my spine.

Nope, nope, I can't think that way. Lexie loves me. She'll understand. We'll be okay. She knows I wanna be there.

Then again, I've stood her up a bunch of times. Can't expect her to tolerate this forever. But it'll be okay. If I can get there in time to give her just one dance, it'll be enough–I hope.

"Come on, bunghole. Ain't gonna...it ain't gonna do it itself." Denver yells from his tow truck throne.

I startle, realizing he's been watching me, ever lurking to make sure I don't get a moment's break. The sun paints his tow truck throne a muted orange gloss, no longer blinding me when I look in his direction. Daylight's dipped below the hills, leaving the yard in long shadows waiting to swallow any remaining light.

I picture my girl on her patio watching the same sunset. My heart aches, knowing how much this must be hurting her. She's counting on tonight being spectacular.

Please don't break up with me over this, Lexie. Please, please, understand one more time.

Sweat beads down me like I'm at a double header on a Saturday afternoon. I'm so thirsty. Starving. Really feeling the fact that I haven't had anything besides half a granola bar.

If the hunger doesn't kill me, Lexie's going to.

Nope, it'll be Bobby. He's gonna kill me for not showing up for her.

And I'm gonna deserve it.

I swear I deserve every bad thing that happens.

"I got prom tonight." I mumble so Denver can't hear, putting my back into the work. I'm so sore from baseball. Three nights of playing and a game in the morning. Didn't need to exhaust my arms and legs any more.

The whole team's resting while I'm here. Missed school for the junkyard. Mrs. Rutherford keeps asking me if everything's okay, and I smile and nod like it is. But it never is. Nothing could be more of a lie.

See, I deserve this hell on earth, because *"Lying lips are abomination to the Lord."* Proverbs 12:22. I'm a liar, and now I'm standing up my girlfriend.

I heft the scrap metal. Almost done going through the section Denver's yelling about.

Better, stronger, faster, more.

My motto gets me through sucky days like this one. One day... Oh, one day, I'll have what I need. I'll be over all my inner demons. The life of my dreams. Play baseball with Bobby. Maybe Lexie and I will have a kid or two if I can figure my stuff out. Or five. I don't know. Something.

Something better than what I have now.

Denver hangs out of the side of the tow truck, belting the words to "Jolene" by Dolly Parton. He drinks. I work.

"Gotta get everythin' moved over! Faster! Faster!" He claps his hands. Heaven forbid he lift a finger on his own pile of garbage.

It's getting hard to see now that the sun's totally set. I squint at the street lamp coming on. Denver's yelling for his dogs that watch the junk after dark. A car passes on the old dirt road, the headlights burning circles of light in my eyes long after it passes.

And I'm not at Lexie's house. Not even close. I have to get to her.

Better, stronger, faster, more.

I haul another load. Mosquitos bite at my skin, despite my best efforts to swat them away.

"Alright bunghole, that's enough."

I tense up, worried I'm doing something wrong. Sweat drips down my forehead, my heart pounding against my hungry chest.

"Got my buddies meeting me at Western Exposition. Can't keep babysittin' ya here all night. Yer just gonna have to...just gonna have to come back later and...and finish all this."

Phew. My shoulders relax. I didn't do anything wrong. Just gotta hear him slurring about getting to his Friday night plans.

I finish the bundle in my arms and head over to his tow truck. Several uncomfortable minutes pass as he keeps yelling hodgepodge lyrics he can't seem to remember.

I stand waiting for the forty bucks for today's work.

"What? Yer bike ain't gonna get ya home?"

"Bike's fine." I look at his boots, all scuffed up. Shivers work down my spine, so stressed about what I have to say. If he was a good uncle, the money would be in my hand and I woulda been on my way hours ago. Heck, if he was a good uncle, he woulda just helped out and gave Mama the cash without making me miss school to work. But he's not. And I have to assert myself against the devil incarnate.

I clear my throat, knowing that it'll fail me if I try to talk without clearing the way for these words. "Ma says you're gonna gimme cash." I don't wanna ask. It's the worst thing. But we need that extra forty or they are gonna shut off the power...again.

"Cash?" Denver spits a wad of tobacco onto my jeans and work boots, just as scuffed up as his are. "I ain't got cash for ya, bunghole."

"But that's the whole reason I've been here." My heart pounds harder against my chest, realizing we're out of earshot.

Denver may not look like much, as drunk as he is now, but I've been on the wrong end of his sledge hammer hands before. He's quicker than he looks, even after all his booze, and knows how to throw his broad frame to hit stronger than his unhealthy body oughta be able to.

If he wants to wallup me for talking back to him he can, and no one will hear it. Not the cottage at the end of the road. Not the old gas station between our dump and here. Not even the moths that keep hovering around the headlights of his tow truck. No one will come to save *me*. No one ever does.

"Yer gonna ask for an ass whoopin'?"

My feet are planted. I'm ready. If he throws a punch, I'll run for the bike. He's super drunk...because he's the kind of guy that drinks beer while exploiting his underage nephew. But I'm fast. It'll give me an advantage. Last thing I'll do is show up to Lexie's beat up. I'm already gonna be pushing it to end up there before the whole prom is over.

Better, stronger, faster, more.

I find some faith to say what must be said. Mama needs that money. It's why I'm working my butt off when I have a baseball game first thing in the morning that I won't get enough rest for. Mama knows that the kiddos aren't gonna sleep well without the air and they're gonna have bad dreams without the lights running. There's not much in the fridge, but that'll go bad too and we can't replace it any time soon. I'm doing this for them. Every bit of this is for them.

I look at Denver, downing another bottle of beer. He and Sperm Donor keep their bodies full of every kind of alcohol. Some good Christian men they are.

"I'm not leaving here without the money." It's another lie. If he goes for a punch, I'll run like my life depends on it.

I worry it might.

Nope, nope, not the time for dramatics, my friend. We're standing our ground with Guzzlehead.

"I missed school by bein' here today. I have to keep the lights on for the girls." I bend my knees a little bit so I'm ready to jump out of the way, hoping he's not gonna follow through on that *ass whoopin'* like the many other times he's beat the ever loving shit outta me.

"Kevin's gonna hear about this." Denver spits tobacco/beer slush.

My back burns, the memory of the worst night I've endured from Sperm Donor's hands. Muscles and bones remember.

"We need the money." I grind my teeth to keep up my nerve, shaking in my boots.

Slowly, Denver pulls out a wrinkled five from his pocket. "It's all I got, boy."

"Five ain't forty."

"You'll get the rest when I've got it to give, bunghole." He lunges toward me. My heart jumps into my throat. I turn and run as fast as I can, get on my bike and pedal away from this dump with his sinister laughter ringing in my ears like a circus clown.

Lexie

W here the fuck is he?

I really wanted to be there more than an hour ago. We only get one prom night and it's half over.

"I'm gonna pick up my girl and we'll meet you all there," he said.

Lies.

All lies.

I've been running like a chicken with my head cut off all fucking day, making sure I was ready. Now, I've been sitting at my house with my stomach grumbling. Guess there was no need to rush at the nail salon, hair dressers, and all-over-fucking-Willardson-South-Carolina to make sure I had enough time.

A whole bottle of hairspray keeps my curls in place. They don't even feel like hair anymore. Just crunchy curls I'm trying not to mess up as I slump into the couch and put pressure on my empty belly. Looking down at my peach colored formal, decorated with bright blue butterflies, I lament the hours Trish and I spent shopping to find the perfect dress. I look amazing. Incredible.

Fuckably gorgeous.

My mind drifts to the constant daydream of Cody giving me more of his luscious cock. While my stomach feels like it's eating itself, my lady places are so hungry to feel him inside. Warmth spreads up my core, fueling my desire. We've only been with each other. And yes, it is sometimes more awkward than anything because we started out as two virgins without much of a clue. But wow, do I need him to fuck the living daylights out of me. Satisfy this urge that only gets stronger the longer I think about him.

My panties get damp while I consider every line of muscles up his six pack and chiseled chest. The way it feels when our skin connects and he holds me. Those arms of his that all the papers talk about. His hair lacing through my fingers while I grip him closer. Lost in daydreams, I feel the ghost of his kisses on my lips, let his breath linger hot on my forehead as he thrusts faster and faster.

Forget the dance, I wanna rip this dress off and pin him against a wall.

At this rate, there may not be a choice.

The ache between my legs intensifies, remembering how good he feels when he enters. My body hums with desire. As much as I'm looking forward to the twirls on the dance floor, I'm most excited about getting him to twirl around with me under my sheets.

If I'm not still furious with him. Jesus Christ, he coulda at least called if he was gonna be late. Bet that phone of his isn't working...again.

Trish keeps texting to see if he's shown up. It was so important to him that we go together, just us.

At least he made it seem like it was.

Just more lies, I guess.

This morning, he didn't show up at school, so I know he's having a bad day. A bad week. *A bad life.* I sigh. We agreed not to worry about all this.

Every time I try to help, he pushes me away. I don't know what a relationship is for if not to share your problems with the other person… or at least have good sex.

I pull out my phone and text him again.

Me: You coming?

Nothing.

I call. It goes straight to voicemail before I hang it up and throw it beside me on the couch. Probably his fucked up phone battery. He'd answer if he could. I know it.

Mom walks past, stopping in her tracks. "What on earth are you still doin' here, Alexia Marie?"

She doesn't tell me I look nice and definitely doesn't make sure I'm okay while I navigate the horrors of high school drama and a boyfriend who likes to make empty promises. Oh yeah, I'd have to have a *real* mother present in my life if I wanted anyone to care about me, instead of this narcissistic excuse for a nurturer.

Her pumps tap the floor, her arms folded tight around her chest. "Answer me."

"Cody was supposed to be here an hour ago." I look down at my dress and throbbing feet in the designer heels Mom picked out. So sick of wearing them, I unhook the buckle and kick them off my feet. "I'll just go paint."

"The hell you will." Mom gives me one of her famous *I'm disappointed in you* glares. *How could you even think such a thing?* She doesn't have to say that part, she already has so many times it's etched forever in my brain.

"Maybe you need to go pick him up. Come on. Go figure out what's keeping him. I'm sure he didn't mean to be late. You're the one sitting on your tush doin' nothing. Come on." The way my parents take his side infuriates me. It doesn't make any sense.

Except that I'm nothing more than their bastard daughter. And he's the next big MLB Pitcher.

Guess it does make sense.

A tightness fills my throat. Why the fuck am I jealous of what they feel for him? My friends would kill for their parents to approve of their boyfriends. Heaven knows Cody deserves a parental figure that appreciates him. I have the life so many would kill for and yet I'm completely miserable.

What am I thinking? Should be counting my blessings. Could I be any more entitled right now? I'm a privileged princess, just like they say.

"Go find him and get to the dance." She raises her eyebrows. *Part of bein' in this family means listenin' to your parents.* The words brainwashed into me since birth remain my reminder that I must, indeed, obey.

"Now." That tone of hers is filled with ice, the way she's talked to me for as long as I can remember.

Two more months and Cody and I move to Suncastle. Our group of friends vowed to go to college together, and since it's the top pick for baseball, that's where we'll be. I wanted to go to the Laguna College of Art and Design, but that's another thing I can't control. Art isn't a reasonable career–according to my parents–and I need to stay flexible so if Cody gets drafted to MLB, I can transfer wherever he is.

Suncastle is going to be perfect, I can feel it. Two hours away from my parents, who control every bit of my existence. As if I wanted them to....

"Now, Alexia Marie Hawthorne, before the chicken lays its last egg." Mom's nagging makes me jump off the couch and get in my SUV.

Thoughts like poison erode my mind with memories of how awful yesterday morning was. I'm not sure how many more toxic fights with my mother I can handle. Though I don't want to let her words harm me, they always seem to. Maybe one day I'll be able to withstand her influence, or maybe I'll always be mad that she sucks at being a mother and blames me for all her mistakes.

Between the drama at home and the reality that my boyfriend's later than a period that causes a pregnancy scare, I seathe the entire drive.

My throat's tight as I park outside of Cody's trailer, knowing that he doesn't like it when I come over–unless we've planned it far in advance.

"It's better to hang at your place." He's told me a million times.

Well, Cody, it's better to actually show up for your date on prom night. Hm, what'd ya think of that?

Hiking up my skirt, I go down the long gravely path to the heap that's anything but a home. I knock for a minute and no one answers. The lights are off.

"Cody? You here? Mama Jones, you home? It's Lexie." I keep knocking. "Mama Jones?"

I'm guessing she's at one of her jobs and the kids are probably at their aunt's house for the night.

Why is this happening? Hasn't this week already been hell enough? I just wanna relax in a bathtub. Hell, I'd wear this dress and soak away all my troubles, fingering all the places I long to be touched.

After waiting in the hot car long enough to make my eyebrows glisten, I figure I've had enough wallowing. Time for a plan.

I'll go to the dance by myself.

My stomach gnaws at the worry of what everyone's gonna think seeing me there alone. It's no secret that Cody and I are together. They're all gonna think we broke up or some shit. I really don't wanna deal with judgemental glares from my peers, I get enough of that at home.

Nothing I can do about it now.

I drive to the fanciest hotel in downtown Willardson. Cars fill the parking lot, and I muster up all the courage I can to get out of the vehicle. I text Cody again.

Me: At Prom...get your ass here.

My throbbing feet take one step at a time into the hotel. I stop along the way to dislodge a pebble that got stuck from Cody's gravel. What the fuck am I doing here alone?

Jason Mraz's "I Won't Give Up" blares out of the ballroom and couples dance across the floor.

Please don't let anyone notice me. Please, God, Jesus, Universe, whoever's out there. Listen to this prayer of mine.

I sigh knowing it's just a matter of time before I face the inevitable. For a moment I stand frozen in the doorway, clenching my hands in and out of fists. My heart blasts in my chest and I pull out my phone to take a selfie with a fake smile. I'll text it to Mom to prove I was here and then get the fuck out.

There's a bench outside of the ballroom and I sit there with another sigh, pulling my phone out again and calling Cody three more times– all going straight to voicemail.

Where is he?

If only this wasn't a common occurrence. Sometimes I wonder what we're doing together. He missed my art gallery exhibit, where my art was the main display. Most people don't get that kind of an honor during their high school career. He's already missed my birthday. Now he's missing prom… Just gonna add this one to the growing list.

Looking at my lock screen and his gorgeous smile, I know. A millisecond in his presence is so warm it's like the home I've never known.

He's probably stuck at work. Damn that phone battery making it so I can't even get a hold of him on a night like this.

I shake my head. He's always working odd jobs trying to have enough cash for food. I told him he could have whatever money he wanted. Of course, he never accepts.

"Lex?" It's Bobby. I'd know that deep voice anywhere. But embarrassment takes hold of me so much that it's hard to look up.

"You wouldn't happen to know where my date is, now would you?" I close my eyes, knowing how horrible that sounds out loud.

"I told him he better make it to this one." Bobby sits by me on the bench. "When he missed class, I texted him but haven't heard back. Maybe he's workin'? Probably. That'd be my guess."

"Is he ever not workin'?" I let out a laugh and it somehow calms my racing heart. Or maybe it's being next to someone who cares.

"He's stupid to not be here for you right now." Bobby's words strike a chord inside of me that I don't want to feel. For a second he looks at me with something in his eyes that I can't quite read. I've known him for years and he's always been awesome. Bobby's good at listening, good at being supportive, and fun to be around. Good at everything, really. There's lots of reasons why he's one of the more popular kids at school.

He wouldn't have stood me up on prom night.

A shudder goes through me at such a strange thought. Girls fall all over Bobby at Willardson High, and why not? He's tall, does his hair, smells like Hollister–where he buys all his clothes, and is crazy talented at baseball. But I've never let myself think of him as anything besides a friend. Considering what going to prom with him woulda been like is plain crazy. He's never flirted with me a bit.

I'm just upset.

Everything's about to change for the better so I can hang on for a little bit longer. Cody won't have to work when he's on scholarship playing baseball. Or maybe he still will need to send money home. I don't know how he's gonna juggle all that.

"Save countin' chickens for the farmers, Alexia Marie. What do you care if they hatch anyhow?" Granna always says. She likes to mix up old sayings like that. My tummy grumbles and I press a hand over it.

"You want some punch? Or water? They have crackers and shit too. Want some?" Bobby offers me his hand, and I take it.

"Yeah, I'm starved." I feel better with him beside me, like even though Cody's not here I'm not all by myself. My knight in black armor.

We get to the refreshments before I realize we're still holding hands. I pull mine away and clench a fist. "Where is your date?"

"Enjoyin' Teddy Hamilton in the parkin' lot, last time I checked."

"Oh, shit." I bring my fingers to my lips.

"Just teasin'." Bobby grins that million dollar smile of his.

I elbow him in the ribs. "Makin' me feel bad for askin' when I'm already showin' up to prom alone." I look up and he shrugs.

I roll my eyes. "I mean it though. Where's your date?"

"Didn't bring anyone." He looks at the room filled with people as we step through the refreshment area.

"No? Pretty sure you had your pick."

"Almost didn't show, honestly." Bobby gets a cup of punch for both of us. "Thought we were all gonna have plans." There's a bit of sadness in his tone and I realize that Cody not being here is a selfish thing that affects more than just me. If he hadn't insisted on picking me up, our friend group woulda gotten together. Bobby and I both wouldn't have had to endure the awkwardness of arriving alone to the biggest dance of our high school career.

"What are you doin' here then? Heaven knows I wish *I* wasn't." I've gotta know. If he didn't bring a date and if our group didn't have plans, why is he here?

"Mom threatened hell if I didn't wear this fancy tux she rented." He clears his throat. "She's pretty pissed I didn't ask anyone to go so I thought I better not push it." There's this funny expression on his face and it makes it feel so much lighter. I don't know why but hanging out with Bobby right now is exactly what I need. I'm already feeling so much better than when I walked in the door.

"Well, my mom insisted I pick up Cody, but he wasn't at his house." I offer my glass of punch for a toast. "To controlling mothers."

He clinks my cup. "I'll drink to that."

I sigh. "Some senior prom."

"You deserve better." Once it's out of his mouth, he pulls his lips tight like he's said the wrong thing. He grips the back of his neck, his words hitting me harder than I knew possible. Forget feeling lighter, I'm now in a freefall.

Every part of my insides burn, because he's just said the fear I've thought a thousand times. Is it really that obvious that he can see? My eyes well up, a rush of pain from all the times I wished Cody could show up for me.

It is obvious. No matter how much I wish it wasn't, other people know. I can hope that it's not everyone. But what if it is?

I stare at him, dumbfounded.

"Deserve better?" My throat is scratchy, wondering why he'd go and say *that*.

"Shit, Lex. I shouldn't tell you this. It's just–" He looks at me for a while, like he's debating something.

"Just what?" I urge, needing to hear the rest, wanting him to take it back. Knowing that he can't, a war battles in my insides, spinning and swirling.

He puts his hands on my shoulders, his eyes kind. "You deserve someone who takes care of you. Cody doesn't."

"He does too." I shake my head emphatically, wondering if I'm more concerned with convincing Bobby or myself. "Cody takes real good care of me when he's around." I put our empty cups on a table. "He's just too busy taking care of others. He stretches so thin that I end up being lower on the priority list. I'm sure it won't always be like this. It's just that I only get what's left of him after all his other responsibilities, and sometimes that's not much." I look down at my shoes, rubbing my feet something awful. There's a tightness in my throat, feeling like I shouldn't be saying anything bad about Cody. I mean, he's not even around. What kind of girlfriend am I?

"You need more than his leftovers, Lex. Like if I was dating him, I wouldn't put up with this." Bobby's eyes hold mine and I know he's looking out for me. If Cody wasn't so incredible, I wouldn't put up with it. But I know he's just going through a lot and he won't take any of my help. The least I can do is be patient with him.

"He's doin' the best he can, I know that. It's enough for me, really." I keep shaking my head, blinking back my filling eyes.

"Okay." Bobby smiles. "I don't wanna stir up trouble for the two of you. He's amazing, I know he is. Just hate seein' ya sad."

He pulls me into a long hug. I inhale his scent of laundry soap and Hollister cologne, feel his strong arms around me. His grasp lingers and I realize I'm not on the verge of tears any longer.

He withdraws, "Can I help somehow? We don't have to stay. Hell, we can hop in my truck and drive around town 'til we find him. If he wasn't at home he may be at Denver's junkyard."

I consider his option but the thought of us leaving right as he gets here has me fretting. "This may sound funny, but do you wanna dance?" I glance at the couples near us.

"Dance?" He seems confused.

"It's stupid, I know. But I've always wanted to dance at prom. Ever since freshman year and I saw all the flyers going up around school."

"Oh, oh, yeah," he nods. "You don't think Cody would mind?"

"I'm just not sure if he's even gonna make it." I glance at my phone one more time. No messages. "You don't have a date, and apparently I don't either." I tilt my head toward the dance floor. Lots of our friends bob and sway, happily dancing to the music.

"I'd be honored to be your fake date for one dance." Bobby takes my hand and there it is–he's showing up for me *again* when he doesn't even have to. He shouldn't have to.

We find a close spot while the song "Chasing Cars" by Snow Patrol comes through the speakers. It's a comfortable pace as we move our feet in step. He lifts up his hand and spins me, my flowy dress flying like I hoped it would. My heart embraces the joy of having what I've wanted for so long. When I come back to him, we're out of step for a few beats until we get back on track.

"Sorry, Lex. I'm not too good at dancin'." He's hesitant to look at me, his cheeks getting a little pink.

"You're doin' fine. It's probably me." I reassure him.

"It's definitely *not* you," he raises his brows. "We may better quit while we're ahead."

"I don't know anythin' you're not good at." I shake my head. "We'll just dance to this one song. You're doin' perfect. Promise."

"Alright, alright." Bobby's face is all nerves as we move, his hands on my hips, my arms on his shoulders. "So, we'll all be at Suncastle. You excited?"

"Can't come soon enough."

Bobby gets closer, like he's holding me. I take his comfort, realizing how upset I still am. This is prom. Cody's supposed to be here. There's no reason that I can think of that makes it okay that he's not.

"Lex?" Bobby's arms keep me close, his mouth whispering into my ear. There's no part of our bodies that aren't connected. We barely move, frozen in this moment.

"Yeah, Bobby?" I wonder what he's gonna say, begging for it to be something that helps. Something that lets me process how fucked up it feels that my boyfriend isn't here.

He kisses my forehead. "I want you to know..." his face falls, hands dropping from my hips so that we aren't holding anymore. "Cody?" There's a shakiness in his voice and I turn. Bobby puts lots of distance between us.

Cody stands by the punch bowl with a scowl, like he's been watching for a hot minute while we danced. Only he ain't happy and that's clear as day. His eyes widen while his brows furrow. He shakes his head like he can't believe it. His gaze locks on the two of us with an intense, fevered stare. Before he takes a step closer, his fist crumples around something he's holding. I look to see what he's just crushed. It's flowers. For me? Yeah, it's a corsage.

He hovers over it in disgust, forsaking it on the ground.

"Hey, baby. Where were you? I've been callin' all night." I go to give him a kiss but he goes right past me, gripping Bobby by the lapels of his rented coat.

"After all we've been through, you think you can go and do this?" Cody yells. They do an awkward dance as Cody shoves him off the dance floor.

"Hold on," Bobby looks frazzled and out of control trying to get his footing.

"What were you thinking? She's mine. You can't have her!" Cody slams him into the wall. Hard. So hard it rattles the table propped against it and some glasses of punch spill. Cody starts throwing punches. Bobby dodges one and raises his arm up to block another one. Cody grabs his arm and drives a punch into Bobby's eye. It hits so hard the back of Bobby's head slams into the wall again. More glasses of punch spill.

What the fuck?

"Hey!" I try to get Cody's attention. "Hey!" I pull his shoulder, but he pays me no mind.

"You stay away from her," he punches Bobby in the nose.

"Dude," Bobby turns his head away, hand ripping out of Cody's grip and going to his nose as it gushes blood all over his nice tux. "Get off me." His words are a blubbering mess with all the blood spattering, but all I can hear is how his voice holds warning, like an unspoken secret. He's unusually calm, considering Cody's outburst, and I feel left in the dark of whatever is between them.

A few people gather around us, including chaperones. Heat goes to my cheeks, horrified at the scene.

Cody lets go of Bobby and steps back, like he's finally come to Jesus about where he is and how it's absolutely not a place for a sloppy fistfight.

Mr. Jenkins goes to Bobby. "Somebody get us a towel!" Blood streams down both Bobby's hands as they grip his nose for dear life.

I run to the refreshment table and get him some napkins.

"You alright, son?" Coach Wayne, the head baseball coach, has his hand on Bobby's shoulder.

Bobby's looking down, blood streaming everywhere. He takes the napkins to his face and rushes out the door.

Mrs. Rutherford is scolding Cody and I wonder if he's gonna get thrown out of the hotel for acting this way. He just got here, and now he's gone and done this. I'm sure they are gonna make him go.

"I know. It was wrong. I know." Cody holds his head in his hands. "Please, just let me stay for a few minutes. Let me make this right. I promise I won't cause any more trouble. Please?"

"But you hit someone." Mrs. Rutherford seems to be trying hard to figure out what to do.

"Look, I shouldn't have. I won't hurt anyone else. Please, just let me stay?" Cody begs the group of teachers that's congregated to this spot.

The music's stopped. Everyone's staring. Vanessa Hodge and Benny Bigelow exchange alarmed glances. They look at me for an explanation I don't have. Andy Smith has his phone out, recording a video. Several other kids start doing the same thing, laughing to themselves. The whole cheerleading team gathers in tight, already gossiping to each other.

What a scene. Can I disappear?

"You attacked another student." Mrs. Rutherford folds her arms with a tight, unyielding glower.

"We've got a game tomorrow," Coach Duncan, the assistant baseball coach says.

"I know we do." Coach Wayne sounds agitated.

Coach Duncan shakes his head. "You think Anderson will be able to—"

"Of course Bobby'll still be able to play. It's just that noses like to bleed. He's fine. You saw him walk outta here. He wouldn't be walkin' if it was bad." The muffled sounds of the baseball coaches drown out the buzzing in my ears. "Somebody needs to check him out. Should we call his father? No, no, let's not get ahead of ourselves." They argue and it all blends together, who's saying what.

"Look, Cody's not gonna do that again alright? Mrs. Rutherford, can't he stay?" Coach Wayne turns to me and my boyfriend-gone-jealous-lunatic. "Right, Cody?"

"Right. I won't. I promise I won't." Cody steps around the teachers and our classmates, like if he stands here any longer he'll lose his cool again.

"Well are you gonna let Cody play after assaulting someone on your team, too? No consequences whatsoever?" Mrs. Rutherford taps her foot like this is all too typical for the jocks to get off with a wrist slap and nothing more.

"We all know that was out of the ordinary." Coach Wayne looks at Cody with compassion in his eyes.

"But what if it becomes an issue? You don't want Mrs. Anderson going all Mama Bear on you like she tends to do. You'll end up with drama for days. And that's if Bobby's doing alright. Someone needs to go check on him."

Mrs. Rutherford has a good point there.

"Do you really think Bobby's mom would go up against Cody for one issue? Could everyone just calm down for a minute?" Coach Wayne raises his hands. "I'm gonna make sure Bobby's okay."

"Alright, but no more problems or he's out of here." Mrs. Rutherford softens her expression.

When I turn, Cody's picking up the corsage off the ground. Looks like some roses from the bushes in his yard tied together with some old yarn, all crumbled up from when he was about to rage.

What just happened? My thoughts swirl around in my head but it's hard to focus.

I feel torn, wanting to check on Bobby but needing to know why Cody would do such a thing. In the time we've been together, he's never so much as poked me. I haven't seen him hurt a fly.

The music starts up again, allowing many of our friends to take the dance floor. Thank fuck they aren't eyeballing us anymore.

Cody steps close, his hair a perfect gold shimmering off the lights. He's in a borrowed suit that looks like something you'd find at a thrift store. On Cody it looks good, like he's wearing a retro suit that is meant to look out of style intentionally. I offered to buy him a tux, but he wouldn't have it.

There's dirt on his neck and his eyes are full of sadness. "Lex." It's like he's trying to smile but it won't quite work. He comes closer, but hesitates, like he can tell I'm a little scared. I swallow hard, not knowing what to do with all the feelings escalating in my system. If I don't find something to steady me, I'm gonna fall over because this whole ordeal just set everything off balance.

I stand there frozen, just looking at him, trying to understand.

He takes another step. I consider moving away, but know that isn't what I want. He stops just short, like he's making sure he doesn't force me into a hug. When I don't jump away, he leans in to whisper in my ear.

"Lex, I'm so sorry." His arms come around me and hold. I'm too stunned to move, assaulted by all that I feel for him. He's my home. My safety. Only what just happened didn't feel safe at all.

I nestle into him, speaking against his chest. "You weren't at school. You weren't at your house. I called a dozen times." I'm talking super fast, my words as frantic as my heartbeat. "I was so worried about you. I didn't wanna worry, but I had no clue if you were okay or why you'd miss this."

"I got some bad news. I'm not myself. I'm so sorry." He whispers into my ear.

"Bad news?" I shiver and he pulls off his coat and wraps it around my shoulders. My comfort. My home.

"My cousin is back at the hospital. I was at the junkyard tryin' to help my uncle."

"You already told me about your cousin."

But that wasn't whatever drove Cody over the edge.

"What was the bad news?"

"You don't need to worry about it. I'll figure it out." He dismisses it so easily that it stings my fragile heart. Why won't he talk to me? I want to communicate and help. He insists on bearing his burdens on his own even when I want to be here. It leaves me feeling shut out of his world.

I look at him for a long time, hoping he'll elaborate. Instead, all I hear is the pounding in my ears.

"I'm so sorry." Cody's eyes meet mine.

"I'm not the one you just punched in the face. Maybe you should be apologizin' to him."

"Yeah." His eyes go wide like he's waking up from whatever nightmare we all just lived. "Bobby? Bobby. Yeah. Of course. Let's go find him." He takes my hand and we go out the door. I wait outside the bathroom where Cody goes to see Bobby.

I'm still floating in some alternate universe, wondering what it is that I'm not understanding. What would ever cause Cody to react like that, and with Bobby of all people?

Did he really think that dance meant something? I dance with all our friends all the time. It was nothing.

What did Cody think we were doing? I've gotta be missing some-thing. Have no clue what it is, but I don't have all the pieces of this puzzle.

I sink into an empty chair, getting a headache from trying to figure it all out.

Bobby

S hit, that hurt. I hold back tears. They keep coming anyway, merging with blood, leaving a metallic trail running down my throat. Sitting heavy in my stomach. I stare in the bathroom mirror, worried I'm gonna heave.

Not now, Anderson. Don't heave right now. It'll just add to the stains on this shirt.

I shouldn't have danced with her. Not when he wasn't around. Had my hands on her hips. Her hands wrapped around my shoulders. There wasn't anything innocent about how that appeared.

Or how it felt.

Why did I kiss her forehead? Before it was a dance, no big deal. But I was holding her. And then I kissed her skin and it changed me. I knew. I've always known there's something here that I desperately want to explore.

I keep replaying that moment like I'm stuck in a hamster wheel. We held each other and talked. It was so natural, even though I can't dance. She's just that goodness in the world that I can never get enough of. Her hips under my hands felt *right*. So right. I just wanted to make her feel better.

This isn't better.

My nose is a steady stream of blood, the red mixing with my tears in the porcelain white sink. Drops everywhere making swirling patterns like one of Lexie's paintings. I've never got a nose bleed this bad.

Woosh, I'm lightheaded when I pick my head up to look in the mirror. I keep rolling up my sleeves, these damn droplets making a mess. Why hasn't it stopped? I'm sure the fact that I'm crying isn't helping.

Just let it out, Anderson. I tell myself. Because apparently getting punched at prom is enough to reduce me to crying like a baby. Thank goodness no one is in this bathroom.

I'm so furious with Cody. First, he stands her up. Then he punches me? I don't care what it looked like. He didn't even ask us what was going on.

Did I deserve this?

I swallow the lump in my throat, more fucking tears burning down my cheeks. Have to gather myself. Doubt I have long. Someone's gonna follow me in here.

It might be Lexie.

Don't know what the hell I'm gonna do if I see her with tears going down my face. Imagining this moment doesn't make me feel embarrassed like I thought it would. No, if she came in here, she'd put her arms around me and hold me while I'm crying. I'm sure of it. There'd be no shame in feeling these emotions that have always run deep within me. She wouldn't shame me for falling apart. She'd understand why. She'd comfort me.

That's part of why I love her so much. I always have. Since the first time I hung out with her I've felt free to be me.

It's like I feel her comfort just by thinking about it.

Jeez Lexie, how do you make me feel so much better when you're not even here?

I let out my first full breath since this crying fit. I'm able to enjoy the inhale of cold air bringing healing to my lungs.

The door hinges squeak and I turn toward the fancy hotel wallpaper. I wipe my eyes, trying to hide the evidence of tears.

"You alright?" Coach Wayne hands me a towel. I look at the towel for a little too long. Haven't a clue what to say. Am I alright? Not really. But I don't wanna say that to Coach.

"Thanks." I set the towel on the counter, not sure where to begin cleaning up this mess. Or maybe it's for my face?

"Want me to call your parents?" Coach steps closer and I can tell he's checking in on my mental state like he always does when someone gets hit on the field.

"No," I sound awfully funny, talking through napkins.

"Lemme see," Coach looks at my eyes. I pull the napkins off a bit but blood's still dripping.

"Op, let's keep those there for another minute." Coach helps me hold the napkins back in place. "You know your name?"

"Anythin' besides Robert." I joke.

"Know where you are?" Coach's going through all the concussion questions I've heard a dozen times. Cody hit me hard, but I doubt I have any brain damage.

"The shittiest prom known to man."

Coach chuckles. "Alright, alright. I think you'll be just fine." He puts his hand on my shoulder. "You sure you don't want me to call your folks?"

"I'm sure." I swallow hard thinking about how they're gonna react. Tasting the coppery tang of my own blood. I need to buy some time before I have to explain all this.

Coach hesitates, looking deeper into my eyes.

"I'll still play tomorrow. I'll go get some sleep and I'll be good to go." Jeez, I sound ridiculous.

"Of course. Well, if you need anything I'll be here." His eyes are concerned. I feel like I'm under a microscope. This is the worst kind of attention.

"Thanks Coach."

He leaves and I stare in the mirror.

I shouldn't have gotten so close to her.

"Looks like *The Shining* in here." Mickey comes through the bathroom door. "Cody did this? I'll go wreck his face."

"No," I force a trembling breath. "I'm fine," I press the tissues harder on my nose. Fuck, it hurts. I shouldn't be surprised Cody can punch...just never thought I'd experience it on my own face.

"You are not fine. He just punched you hard enough that your brains are leakin' out of your nostrils." Mickey looks at me with disbelief in his expression. "Aren't you gonna fight back? Or at the very least ask me to?"

"Look, it's done. Can you go see if Lexie's okay?" I clear my throat, tight with emotion and all the blood I'm swallowing. My mouth tastes like a morgue.

"Lexie? Why wouldn't she be okay?" Mickey's anger is evident in his tone, making all of this hit harder. "He didn't hit–"

"No, of course he didn't hit her." Jeez, it sounds awful coming from my lips.

"But he hit you." Mickey's pacing and it's not helping me calm down. "What would be wrong with Lex?"

"I don't...I don't know. Look, I don't know. Okay? It probably freaked her out. Just go make sure she's alright while I get cleaned up." I pick up the towel from Coach.

"Okay..." Mickey leaves me alone in the bathroom.

My body feels so weak, like my heart's been beating too hard for too long. The life's been sucked outta me. All I can do is collapse to the cold tile floor and lean against the wall.

But he hit you.

And now everyone knows. Because we couldn't get into this fight privately. No, it had to be in front of the whole fucking school. At least all he did was hit me. Who knows what woulda happened if he yelled about....

No, no. Not gonna think about that. Can't think about that. Didn't happen. We agreed.

The door squeaks open again, because apparently this was enough to cause a scene and everyone is gonna come make sure I'm alive in this restroom.

Only, it's not Coach or any of the other chaperones. I know who it is, and I'm not ready for it.

I close my eyes, wishing to be anywhere but here.

Cody

The weight of everything crashes against me as I see Bobby on the floor.

What have I done?

I hurt him. Bad. I clobbered my best friend.

Muscles and bones remember.

My hands shake as my eyes dart around the room. The blood everywhere registers the magnitude of how hard I hit him.

I lashed out. I lost control. I became a bully. A monster. Don't know what was going through my head. I'm the one that should be bleeding on the cold marble tile.

It's just us. Alone. How I should've talked to him in a reasonable way instead of losing myself to the rage inside me, in front of all our friends no less.

I'm just as jacked up as my father. Kevin, the psychopath. Kevin, the deranged creature whose lack of self control led to my own birth, along with at least seven other kids that we know of. Kevin, my worst enemy.

Nope, I'm *more* jacked up than Kevin. Because he's never hit me in front of everyone. Always in secret. Behind closed doors where no one could hear my screams.

My back burns, the beating that always haunts me. The one I vowed would be the last one I'd take. But oh, how I deserve one now.

Is Mrs. Rutherford gonna call my parents? My mouth goes dry at the thought. Denver's gonna tell Kevin all sorts of stuff from me talking back to him. If that compounds with trouble at school....

A wave of panic blows through my system, making me numb all over. I've never been in this much trouble. I have to be good. Have to keep the peace. I get beat even when I don't give him any reason. Now, he'll have reasons.

Blood drains from my head making me feel dizzy. I wanna run away now and forget everything. But Bobby. And baseball. Of course Lexie. Can't leave all this even if things get bad.

Why is Lex the last thing I think about?

Cody, quit being so selfish! We're here to check on Bobby and then go dance with Lexie. Now, make all of this right. There's still time!

Soreness in my legs makes me remember the hell of the last hour. Leaving the junkyard, I rode my bike so fast for five miles to my house. Every circle of the pedals made my legs throb but I kept going. No one was home since Mama's working and Anna Mae's too young to watch all the kiddos alone. I scrubbed off super quick, racing to get dressed and grab some flowers from the yard. Pedaled another three miles on throbbing legs to get to her. All for her. My Lexie.

She was gonna drive us once I got to her house, but I ended up bumming a ride off Mrs. Hawthorne with my bike in the back of her Cadillac Escalade.

And I got here. Just in time to see *them.*

He kissed her. In front of me. Without knowing I was here. So really, it was behind my back. What else are they doing behind my back?

How could he do that? To me? To us? How could he?

Nope, nope, this ain't his fault. It's mine. I never shoulda hit him.

But he was the one dancing with her.

Nope, nope, we aren't gonna blame him. That's what Kevin would do. We will not be Kevin. We have to be better than that, Cody.

Only, I'm not, and that's clear as the picture in front of me.

My wobbly knees make it hard to stay standing still. I wanna curl up next to him and we can wallow in the misery I caused. Bobby gets it. Sometimes I swear we share the same soul. I've shattered both of ours tonight.

He stays still, head down, eyes closed. Maybe he's praying. Though I've stood here a while, there's nothing that makes him look up. Is he trying to ignore me?

Please, Bobby, don't push me away. I know, you have every reason to. But please, don't.

What if this is it? What if I've *really* done it this time? We've had our moments in the past. But what if I went too far?

Quit being so flipping selfish Cody!

There's an ache spreading around my chest as I consider what life will be like if he really ignores me. What if he doesn't let me apologize? That'll be worse than a bad night with Kevin. I can handle my deadbeat father, it's what I've always had to do. But I can't handle the possibility that I messed up with Bobby.

I've really done it now. Ruined everything.

That's all you do. Kevin's taunting voice rings in my ear.

I turn to go. There's nothing I can say to fix this. Nothing I can do to change the way I've destroyed him. Destroyed us.

"Wait," Bobby sniffles.

The sound hits my ears and I can tell he's trying to be strong for me. This is the hope I need. My feet stand frozen on the tile. He doesn't want me to go. That's crazy. Of course he does. Why the heck would he wanna talk to me? The only reason to tell me to wait is so he can get his payback.

Only, Bobby's not like that. Even when I'm a crazed demon. He's gonna let me explain, I can feel it. This is the biggest rift I've ever caused, but I think *maybe* we can still fix this. Fix us.

"Hold up," he coughs, clearing his throat.

Everything about my yearning heart melts at the sound. He does wanna talk. He'll know how to mend us. I feel it in my bones. This isn't it. Bobby will save me from myself, like he always does.

Another sniffle. Like he doesn't wanna cry in front of me. Like he doesn't wanna make this about him. Like he just wants his nose to stop bleeding so we can get back to having a good time. He's trying so hard to be strong.

I wanna tell him he doesn't have to. Because when it's us, we can be who we *really* are.

Bobby

Scuffed up loafers, with a bunch of hardened mud, stand still as the door hitches closed. I can't look at him. Not now. Not after what just happened. Not after knowing that I'll just live the rest of my life acting like nothing happened.

He turns to go. I wonder if he will. Keep running. Always running from the truth. From the pain.

If I was him, I'd be running too.

"Wait," I press the tissue tighter to my nose. "Hold up," I sound so fucking awful. Jeez. I cough out the blood and phlegm stuck in my throat.

He comes close. The scent of Zest soap is so strong that even through my mangled nose and waded napkins, I inhale the familiar smell. Trying to mask the grease and dirt that won't come clean. I've seen how it lingers on his skin for a while. Like he never can get the grease washed clean after working at the junkyard.

My stomach drops, realizing that must be where he's been. That's why he almost stood up Lexie. No wonder he wasn't at school. That uncle of his makes him drop everything to come and work. I've never understood why his mom lets him miss school. My folks would go nuts if I botched up my perfect attendance record.

Cody's knees hit the ground next to me and I see a dirty spot he forgot to scrub on his neck. Reminds me of when we'd spend all day playing ball and dirt stuck to our sweaty skin. Wish we woulda been at the field. Wish he coulda been anywhere besides the junkyard. Wish I woulda gone and helped him.

"I didn't mean to, Bobby. I didn't...I just...I've ruined everythin'." He sounds like hell. There's a bunch of bug bites starting to turn pink on his tan skin. A touch of a sunburn colors his cheeks and forehead. His stomach grumbles. He doesn't have to tell me that he's skipped supper. Probably hasn't eaten all day.

I wanna tell him to fuck off. Wanna tell him that was too far. Wanna tell him how much I miss the friendship we used to have, the one that's completely obliterated now. How I wish it was just the punch.

Lately, he's only been hanging with Lexie. Not much with me. I don't wanna drift apart. That's all he's been doing. I remain here ready and waiting for him to remember me. This oughta be the last straw to break our friendship. He's been treating me like shit for months.

We are through, Cody. Friends don't act like this.

It's on the tip of my tongue. Where it'll stay.

I can't let him go. Not even over this. Because I get it.

I get the *why* of his behavior. Somehow, that makes it easier to forgive him.

I probably shouldn't.

There's a burning in my throat, mixing with how bad my nose throbs. It takes several seconds before I offer a quivering, "I know."

His arms come around me in a hug both loving and sorry. My breath hitches as I fold into his tight grasp, holding the napkins to my nose. I linger close. Trying to let him take this pain away. Knowing he can't.

He hurt me. And this isn't the first time.

This won't be made right. But it doesn't have to be. I'll just absorb it, like I always do. Guess that's why we're good for each other. Or maybe it's why we're bad.

He causes problems. I take them all on so that he doesn't have to add to the weight he always carries. Already know his shoulders bear too much. So I take this on, trying to make life better for him. I just wanna help.

"I didn't mean any darn bit of it." He holds me tighter, begging with all that he is for my forgiveness. "I don't wanna hurt you anymore."

"I know, I know." I pull back to see his eyes, full of regret. "I won't dance with her again."

"I shouldn't have raged on you."

"My nose agrees." I pull the wadded napkins away long enough to see that the blood has finally come to a clot.

"I'll help you find a replacement best friend. I'm sure Mickey would love the new position. He's been vying for the promotion like a secretary eyes the delivery man for a little treat behind the watercooler–"

"What the heck are you talkin' about?" I chuckle, and it hurts my raw throat.

"Ya know, the type...always tryin' to get close to you. Always lookin' at you like you're the coolest one in this school–"

"I *am* the coolest one in this school and you know it." I cut Cody off. Or did we both lose popularity for that fight?

"Second coolest. I'm first. But seriously, how about you let me set you up with the next best buddy you deserve and then I'll just give you that space and we can say hi in the hallway every second Tuesday of the month or somethin'. We'll work it out...yeah, we'll work out somethin'."

"Every second Tuesday, huh?" I laugh, but it turns into a hiss and a wince since my nose is jacked up. "Nah, how about you just don't punch me again?" I meant it lightly, but he takes it hard, the mood shifting.

"I won't," he looks at his shoes, the reason why I forgive so easily written all over his face. "It was wrong. I know it was wrong and I wish I could take it back." His eyes go to the wad of napkins I'm holding. "Can I get you some ice or somethin'?" It's more a joke than a real question. I know he's referencing last fall when he was hurt real bad. He turns the corner of his lip, "Or Mama always has frozen peas for this kinda thing."

I wanna go back to that day, under our peach tree. Life felt a lot easier then. Now we've had this hell of a night. Why can't I turn back the clock to before he and Lexie got together?

"You don't have to put up with it." He looks so lost and broken.

"With what?"

"With me." He throws his hands in the air. "You don't have to let me come in here and apologize and then pretend it's all good. Because it's not!"

He's flipped a switch inside my soul. Pushed my button. Anger boils through me at his tone and his raised voice. I'm doing the best I can. Everything about this night is wrong. Now he's yelling at me?

"What do you want me to do?" I'm so fucking intense right now. Zero to a thousand. My heart pounds in my chest. "You want me to blow up? You wanna hash this all out? We both know you had a shit day. That doesn't mean you get to hit me!" I'm yelling louder than he was. No, this isn't what I want.

"Hit me back!" His eyes well up, squaring his shoulders like he's ready to take my hit.

"I don't wanna hurt you," I grab a wad of his shirt, bringing him close to me. "And I don't wanna talk about it anymore. Hitting you back doesn't make it right."

"No, it doesn't." He blinks a few times and I realize that my eyes are welling up with him.

"And it doesn't mean you get to do it again." I let go, realizing I'm holding us really close.

We sit for a while, the only sounds are our heavy breaths.

"I asked Lexie to wait in the hallway. We better not keep her waiting." He stands up and offers me a hand. I go to the sink and wash away the blood as best as I can.

"Mom's not gonna like this." I stare at the stains forming on my shirt.

"Switch me." He starts to unbutton, golden chest hair and defined pecs sticking out from below his third button.

"No." I put my hand on his, stopping him. "She'll know it's not from the rental place. I'll take it to get it dry cleaned or somethin'."

"Lex will know what to do." Cody's confidence sends a pang through me. Of course she will. She's bailed us out of more shenanigans than I can count. And he's the one that gets to have her. When most of the time, it's his damn fault she has to fix things.

"We're cool, right?" His eyes hold mine.

"Yeah, we're cool." I try to sound convincing. Because we are. I know we are. Never have been able to hold anything against him.

But this is the first time something big has come up since he and Lexie got together.

Except what happened that one night...

No, no, not gonna go down that path. The past is in the past. I need to leave it there and forget it. And I will. One day. He didn't mean the hurt he caused that day, either.

Gotta focus on now. On the future. On what's best for Lexie and Cody.

Still, these memories stir. What if they aren't right for each other?

Just let it go, Bobby. I grit my teeth. Jealousy isn't productive. It won't change a thing. Tuning into the meditation I did this morning, I work to ground myself. They're in a relationship. I have to move on.

Only, I've been trying to do that for the last nine months.

It's not working.

Especially not after we danced.

Lexie

They finally come out. Cody's arm is hooked around Bobby and they're smiling, joking around. This makes me even more confused.

"You okay?" I ask Bobby, worried that this violence may be *normal* for them when I'm not around.

"Lexie, darlin', we're gonna need your help because of all the places I could've hit Bobby, I clearly picked wrong." He looks at me for a minute and then tilts his head for Bobby to explain what he's talking about.

"Does he have a head injury? Do we need to get him to the hospital?" My mind goes to the worst case scenario. I've been studying up on all kinds of sports medicine stuff, following around the athletic trainer at the high school, so I know if someone gets hit just right it can really mess them up.

"Oh, nope, his head's fine." Cody sounds sure.

"Although, Mom's gonna have my head over this." Bobby looks at the blood stains and I think about how his mom is a clean freak.

To controlling mothers....

"Ohhhh," I start to connect the dots. "You sure you're okay though?" I look at his pupils, determining if they're equal, round and reactive to light. Yep.

"I think I'm okay." He offers a small smile, but then looks over his shoulder at Cody. They're acting so weird tonight. I don't get it.

"Here, let's go wash it at my place." I don't want him getting into any more trouble when it was my idea to dance.

But it wasn't my idea for Cody to clobber his face, Holy God.

"Hey," Trish walks by with Jimmy Hendricks. Been wondering where they were. Looks like they got lost in a back hallway with the way she's glowing. Sure coulda used her support during that tense moment.

"Love this dress, girl. I told you it'd be perfect." She eyes me up and down.

"Yours too!" I bring her into a hug, our shimmery fabric dancing in the lights.

"Was wondering if you were gonna show." She elbows Cody.

Cody rolls his eyes.

"Jesus, Bobby, what happened to you?" Trish's eyes go wide.

"Nothin'." Bobby says and I choose not to make a big deal. She'll know soon enough. I'm sure everyone's gonna be posting the videos online. We'll never live this down.

"We're going to my place to wash up Bobby's shirt. Y'all wanna come by?" I'm more than ready to get outta here.

"Think we're gonna be at the Holiday Inn, since this place is crazy money for just one night," she winks at Jimmy, "but thank you."

"Oh, okay. Have fun," I give her another hug and walk with Cody and Bobby to my car. "You just got hit real hard, maybe you shouldn't drive yet." I look at Bobby.

"She's right. We'll come back for the truck." Cody opens the door to the backseat and though I wonder if he's gonna argue, Bobby just climbs in and buckles his seat belt.

"Load your bike up." I pop the back of my SUV and Cody lifts his beat up bike into the back, like we've done a hundred times.

"One sec." He opens Bobby's door. "She deserves one full proper dance, while we're still technically at prom. You alright to wait a bit?"

"Go for it." Bobby nods.

"One proper dance, huh?" I'm not sure what he means. We've already left and I have no desire to be back in that room so long as I live. "It's really okay."

"Nope, it's not." He takes both my hands in his. "I am so sorry I wrecked prom." He brings his forehead to mine, scooping me into his embrace. "Can I dance with you?"

My ears strain to catch the drifts of music when the doors open and close from the hotel. "In the parking lot?"

"Yeah, babe. Why not?" He moves his hands to my hips, leading me in a goofy dance around the car. There's no music, so he starts humming.

"Is that from "The Sound Of Music"?" I try to figure out the tune.

"The only VHS tape at my house that ain't broke." He lifts his hand and I spin. "What? You want somethin' else?"

"Nah. You're the music. I don't need any humming."

"Nope, babe, you're the music. Not me." He smiles big enough I see his eyeteeth. Reminds me of the night we first went out on a date. He was all smiles. Flirting with me like crazy, making me feel so important. And here it is, all the reasons why I love him circling this moment like the cold air circles our bodies.

He lifts his arm up and I spin again and again, my dress flying in the cool South Carolina breeze. My tight chest loosens, releasing the tension I've been holding all afternoon. This is finally our moment. I'm with my Prince Charming and he's giving me the dance of my dreams. Everything about it is perfect and magical.

His smile warms my insides, that wanting to be near him intensifying with each step. Every breath feels more and more like coming home. He is my home. I'm glad he's happy again. That moment in the dance was so hideous but he and Bobby have moved on and so can I.

A yawn comes out of my mouth before I have time to hide it. Like the whole day has caught up with me, I'm straining against heavy eyelids.

"You're not already gettin' tired are you?" He's teasing me with his tone, with his eyes. "I've got a lot planned for later, so you can't be tired yet."

"Maybe I'll stop for a coffee." I giggle, realizing that I am insanely exhausted.

"There ya go. A double latte." He spins me again and I flutter like the butterflies on my dress.

"I don't know how you do it." I laugh.

"Do what?" He gives me a confused expression.

"Get away with standing me up at prom."

"This, my sweet, is just the appetizer for me getting away with standin' you up for prom. We're gonna have to fix this. For real. More than a little dance in the parking lot. I'll think of somethin'." He winks.

"You always do." I hold him close and we sway. "But what really happened? Are you and Bobby okay?" My eyes find Bobby laying down in the backseat of my SUV with his arm over his face, blocking the little bit of light from the parking lot. He looks absolutely miserable, and maybe a little pale. I think about the way he held me so close and kissed my forehead. I know he just meant it as friends, but his body's paying quite the price.

"It was a sucky day. And I wish it wasn't today, but it was." Cody's face tells me that's all he wants to say, when I know there's a hell of a lot more.

"You know I wanna help. I wanna actually be there for you. Like most people let their girlfriend be." I've said this a dozen times, the same argument over and over.

"Babe, you are." He brings his lips to mine, a kiss so deep and passionate it takes my breath away.

Bobby

He's dancing with her outside of prom.

What is this? An eighty's movie? He might as well be outside of her house with an old school boombox blaring "In Your Eyes" by Peter Gabrial. Too bad I'm not John Cusack and we aren't gonna end up together.

She's smiling so bright. I wish it was me.

It's not.

Never gonna be.

I lay down for a while, the throbbing in my head bad enough to make me nauseous. My phone buzzes in my pocket. Heart pounding as I see Vanessa's name appear. I click to read the text.

Vanessa: You okay?

Me: Yep. Thanks.

Vanessa: What do you want me to tell everyone? Do we hate Cody now?

Me: No, God no. Tell them it's fine.

SHE'S TALKING ABOUT THE CHEERLEADERS AND JOCKS IN THERE gossiping up a storm after our scene. Vanessa dictates who's who at the school. One day she convinced everyone to stop talking to Chuck since he did some way not cool shit. We all listened to her. She has that kind of power in the high school hierarchy.

If I wanted to, right now I could sway the vote. Make them hate Cody. He'd lose his popularity in a heartbeat after something like tonight. Sure, he's the most popular kid at school. But they saw something horrific. And horror scares people. Scared people act impulsive. Impulses to shun isn't something people recover from, either.

This could be his fall. His demise.

I could trigger it.

The power is almost tempting. Emphasis on almost. I'm not like that. Normally he's not like this either.

They'd avoid him even this close to graduation. He'd lose all his friends and status. A pain grows in the pit of my stomach. I can't let that happen. We all make mistakes.

He'd better not hit me again, though. This is a one time allowance. Never again will I forgive behavior like this.

I hope.

Not knowing stirs up a really icky fear inside of me. Will I keep putting up with this if it's the new normal? My eyes burn at the thought. Wish I could calm my racing mind. I don't know why he lost it tonight. But he's already trying to fix things.

I look at him dancing with her. Love seeing him able to give her something, especially after everything else.

Vanessa: Andy videoed the whole thing. You wanna see?

I hold my eyes closed tight. Video? Fuck no.

Me: Please have him delete it.

Me: I swear this could really fuck us over.

Me: You've gotta do me this favor.

Me: Don't let anyone post it. It never happened.

Clicking send before I finish my thoughts is impulsive but I've gotta make sure she knows this is urgent. I'm typing so fast my fingers keep sliding over the wrong buttons and I have to correct them.

What if she can't do anything? What if this gets to all the baseball higher powers that be? What if it ruins us? Ruins Cody?

Fuck, I'm gonna throw up. My stomach cramps up and bile rises in the back of my throat. No, not here. Throw up in the back of Lexie's car? Not hot.

I swallow it down, trying not to gag. This can get us both into real trouble. Guilty by association.

Vanessa: I'll see what I can do.

Slowly, I'm able to convince my body to calm the fuck down. I start to relax knowing Vanessa well enough that she means it. Thank goodness I'm in with the in-crowd or this would be too far gone for anyone to repair. She can probably nip this in the bud, fast.

Cody runs around to open the door for Lex. I release a heavy breath, sitting up to get buckled. Still nauseous but not puking.

When they finally get settled in the car, Lexie's giggling and catching her breath.

Don't look at her. Don't look at her. Don't look at her.

I look at my shoes.

I look at my phone.

I look at the back of the seats.

I look out the window.

My eyes keep pulling toward her. I can't let this show. I can't. Cody's already lost his shit tonight. I don't wanna push him any farther.

Why didn't I just hit him back?

One, my old man would lose his shit over that.

Two, I'm already in enough trouble over this shirt.

Three...I just can't hit my best friend.

But he can hit me?

I know, I know.

At least I won't be caught hitting someone on camera if for some reason Vanessa can't track down all the videos. God, I hope she can.

I close my eyes. She laughs. I feel that laugh through every part of me. I wanna just go home. But no, we need to get this stain out.

More than the stain, Mom will wanna know what happened. Then one question will lead to more questions. I cannot deal with that right now. I just got punched by my best friend for dancing with his girl-friend. Repeat, I just got punched by my best friend for dancing with his girlfriend.

Jeez, maybe my head did get a little jacked up. That's why I'm letting her drive. I'm not feeling so hot in the back of this car. But how could I? It's not my head that's broken, it's my heart.

I want what I can't have, sitting right in front of me.

Lexie turns onto her street. I'll get through this without looking at her. I know I can.

What other choice do I have?

She's not mine.

We get to her house and take our shoes off in the entryway. They've got such a nice place.

"Baby girl, is that you?" To our left, Lexie's dad comes out of an office wearing a suit.

"Hey, Daddy." She raises up on her toes and kisses his cheek.

"Didn't expect you back so soon." He says.

"Change of plans." Lexie grabs both of our hands and takes us upstairs in a hurry. "The sooner we get this under water, the better."

"Strip." Cody chuckles while I shed my jacket.

"You got a t-shirt, Lex?" I'd rather not walk around in just these dress slacks.

"Yep." She runs into her room.

"Feeling shy with her now, are you?" Cody says. "You want help?" In a dramatic way, he starts unbuttoning my buttons and I flick his hands away.

"I got it. Jeez, would you keep your hands to yourself?" I set the tie with my jacket and vest, looking it over to see that it's got stains too. Fuck.

"Here, Bobby." She hands me the shirt and I duck into the hall bathroom and shut the door. It's a grey pajama shirt with Care Bears on it. Fits me snug. It's super soft, like she has slept in it a thousand times. Probably the biggest shirt she has. I'm way too tall for it. But it's soft and it smells like her. I hold it against my face and breathe. Before I know it, my face is burning from where it's still fucking tender. Asshole really did a number on my face. God above what was he thinking?

He wasn't.

I smooth the shirt as far down as I can, trying to tuck it into my suit pants. If I hike them up a little bit, it sorta works. Shoulda just gone home. Even Mom's interrogation sounds pleasant compared to how this night's going.

I open the door to the two of them making out against the hallway wall.

"Like I said, water." Lex pulls back from Cody's lip lock and squeezes beside me in the bathroom. She turns on the water and we stand there waiting for what feels like a million years while it does little for the stains.

"I can call my mom to pick me up." I stand outside the bathroom, giving Lexie more space. "Get out of your way."

"No, you don't need to go." She looks up from the sink.

"Yeah, Bobby, we don't want you to go." Cody licks his lips, decorated in Lexie's lipstick. Cody and Lex want me to stay. All I wanna do is disappear. Let this night melt into a past I choose to forget.

"It's prom night. I don't need to be your third wheel." I tug on the shirt that's already riding up.

"You're not a third wheel." Cody's eyes find mine, sincerity in his reflection. "You're never a third wheel, Bobby."

I force a breath, trying to believe him.

Lex runs my shirt under the faucet but the blood's barely fading from a deep reddish brown to a lighter version of whatever that color is. "Let me get the stain stick."

Cody's sitting on the carpet, propped up against the wall. "Please, don't go. I think we're just gonna chill anyway. You wanna chill with us?"

"I...I dunno." I grab the back of my neck, rubbing out the tension. "My headache is getting worse. Probably need to lay down."

"I'm such a dick." He hangs his head.

I sit next to him on the floor. "I get headaches anyway."

"This one's 'cause of me." He lets out a breath. "Please, don't go. Let us take care of you. Let me fix it."

I look into his eyes and they almost make me feel better. What if this is what we need? Maybe if things hadn't been so off lately, that incident at prom wouldn't have happened. I miss my friend. Shit, I miss him so much. Sitting here on the floor, talking like we always do, makes me realize just how hard it's been without him.

"I know you had a long day."

"Got that right." He rubs his thighs. "Hopin' I can even walk tomorrow."

"You could relax with her in the bath." I stretch my shoulders on the doorframe, shocked that I'm suggesting this. Imagining this.

"We can all go get in the hot tub." He pulls my arm to give it a better stretch. Can't count the times we've done this for each other.

"And wear what? Lexie's bikinis?" I look down at how not-well this care bear shirt fits. "I bet she only has those thong ones. Imagine all this in a thong. Yeah, no."

He chuckles at the picture I've conjured up. "There's always skinny dipping."

"With the two of you making out? I don't think so." I glance at the sink, wishing the stains away. Mom's gonna freak.

"It's tempting, though?" he winks.

"Tempting." I smile, trying to relax. To take this moment as it is. We're hanging out. Can't remember when we last got together outside of school, work or baseball. Instead of the mood being so heavy, I'd like to enjoy the night. It's time for a shift. Time to get through this emotional bullshit. I'm done. We're gonna have fun. Headache or not, I'm gonna stay.

"I'll throw it in the washing machine. I think we have some of that dryclean in the dryer stuff for the tie and vest." Lexie's back, messing around with the shirt.

"Thanks." I try to smile, but not for too long. This is so fucking awkward.

Cody's stomach grumbles. "I'm gonna go raid her fridge. Come with?" He looks at me. I look down at the Care Bears shirt.

"You look fine. It's just Lexie's folks anyhow. They're like bats. Never come out of their caves." We walk down the stairs. "Gosh, I'm so sore." He bends to stretch out his hamstrings and I press on his back to deepen the pull.

"Then rest, would you? I don't wanna see us choke out there tomorrow because you're too strained to play."

"I'll be fine by then." Opening the fridge, he gets the gallon of milk and chugs from the jug. "Want some?" he wipes drops off the side of his chin, holding the milk out for me.

"You missed a little bit."

"Here?" He's swatting around like he can't quite feel where the trail of milk led.

"No, over here, you dork." I take my thumb and clean up off his collar bone where there's a trail leading to his chest.

Feels better now. Like we've both cooled down from all the tension. The top two buttons of his dress shirt are undone, his tie loose around his neck. Surprised he doesn't have clothes here.

"I missed a little bit? Then why's it takin' you so long?"

"Missed a lot a bit. Jeez, if you'd slow down maybe some of that milk coulda actually got in your mouth. Let me show you how it's done." I go to the cabinet for a glass and pour.

"Oh, showin' me up all proper like." Cody sits on the countertop.

"Someone has to."

"Y'all want some pizza?" Lex holds out the takeout menu for Pizza Hut. "Here, you want this?" She hands me an ice pack.

"Please," I put the milk jug in the fridge and hold the ice against my face.

She puts the phone to her ear and orders. "It'll be here in half an hour. Y'all wanna watch a movie?"

"Yeah, that sounds great." Cody heads down the hall to their home theater. I follow at a far distance, still feeling that pulsing pain all through my skull.

I wish everything about this moment were different. I coulda asked Vanessa to come with me so I'd at least have my own date. Or even Mickey. Something to take the attention off of me. More importantly, something to take my attention off of them and all I cannot have.

There's shelves lining one of the walls with all the Blu-ray discs in alphabetical order, by genre. Leave it to her family to be cutting edge. We've still got DVDs at my house. But it looks like the Hawthornes not only have a new Blu-ray player, but they've bought every movie on Blu-ray–getting rid of the DVDs.

Extravagance.

"Bobby, you pick." Cody plops into one of the leather recliners, propping up his feet. "I don't care what we watch."

"Do you care, Lex?" I look at her while she turns on the projector.

"I'm good with anythin' you want."

I hand her *Superbad*. We all laughed a bunch when we went to see it in the theater. Our first rated R movie without a parent. Finally getting that freedom we've been itching for for ages. Hopefully it's still funny on the replay.

For a moment, I don't let go of the Blu-ray. Our hands brush against each other and I feel it. What I always feel for her. My heart *wants* her.

Swallow it down, swallow it down. Swallow every feeling down.

I sit in the recliner on the other side of the room.

"Come on, Bobby. You're like across the world from us. You can't see from over there." Cody pats the recliner next to him.

"Just givin' y'all space." I get up and sit where he wants. Guess I'm too tired to fight him on it. It's not worth the drama I'll avoid by just listening.

Cody reaches next to him and gets a blanket out of the basket. He drapes it over all three of us. Lexie snuggles all cozy into his chest.

It's like I can't hear the movie. My head is pounding still.

The doorbell rings for the pizza. Lex pushes pause and we go down to the kitchen where her dad sets the food.

"Pizza on prom night, huh? You coulda ordered from the steakhouse, darlin'." He looks at Lexie.

"The steakhouse doesn't have good wings." She shrugs.

"Fair enough," he chuckles. "Now don't have too much fun, you three." He nods in our direction.

"Goodnight, Mr. Hawthorne!" Cody yells as he leaves down the hall.

"Here's some plates." Lexie sets a stack next to the pizza. We dish up and start eating. Shit, this pizza tastes amazing. All the greasy goodness I was eying on Jimmy Hendrick's plate at lunch yesterday. Didn't realize how starving I was. Supposed to be carb loading for tomorrow. This is perfect.

My phone buzzes in my pocket and I open up a text.

Mom: Mrs. Rutherford called!?!? ARE YOU OK????

Me: I'm fine. At Lexie's house.

Mom: Why didn't YOU tell me???

"Aw shit." I close my heavy eyelids wishing this wasn't happening. She's pulling out all caps. Guess I could've texted her about it.

Mom: I'll come get you.

Mom: We'll stop by the ER. Dad can meet us there.

Mom: Just stay where you are. I'll be right over.

Me: No, please don't.

"Freakin' heck." I drop my phone on the counter.

"What?" Cody looks concerned.

"Mrs. Rutherford went and called my mother." I rest my head against the cold granite counter. "I'm so screwed."

"Why? You didn't do anything." Lexie's standing next to me. "We'll get the stain out before you go."

"Since I didn't tell her, she's freakin' out. Look." Passing my phone to Lexie, I grind my forehead into the cold counter. It feels nice. Like a cold cloth when I have a migraine. Maybe I should ask her for another ice pack since I've melted the first. Jeez, this headache is awful. Mom finding out about tonight is making it worse.

"Op, Mama's callin'." Lexie passes the phone into my hand.

"Gosh darn it," I hurry out of the kitchen to the back porch. "Hello?"

"He hit you?" Mom's frantic. "Why didn't you tell me? Why did I have to hear it from your teacher? Robert Grant Anderson you know that if you ever get hurt–"

"I'm okay, Mom, I promise. It's not so bad. I'm alright. Don't need a doctor." I sink into the lawn chair, rubbing my temples. "I got a nose-bleed and a headache. That's all."

"You sound hurt. Can I come over? Pick you up? At least let Dad look at it. He's in surgery but not for much longer. I already called and I can have him leave work and meet us at the urgent care."

"No, please don't have him leave work. It's not that bad."

Her tone drops low, like a whisper. "What happened that made Cody hit you?"

Nausea bubbles up my throat. Need to avoid all this. It's too soon. "Can we talk about it later?" Peering in through the sliding glass door I see Lexie making out with Cody again. Maybe I should just go.

"Mrs. Rutherford said the punch took you out." Mom sounds like she's crying. Oh, fuck.

"Don't cry, Mom. It didn't take me out. You know Mrs. Rutherford. She's all dramatic. He punched me but we've moved on. It's all good."

The screen door screeches open. Cody walks over. *"You okay?"* He mouths.

I nod. He sits beside me and takes the phone.

"Look, Mrs. A, I didn't mean to and I'm soooooooooo sorry. But it's prom night. Can you please let Bobby hang out with us for a little bit?" Cody sounds like he's trying to charm my mother. Let's just dig the hole deeper, shall we?

"What are you doin'? Give it here." I snatch the phone from his hands. "Mom, I'll text you when I'm on the way home. Please stop worryin' so much. I'm fine. Promise."

"You didn't go unconscious?" There she goes, making a big deal.

"No, I've been conscious the whole time. Coach checked me out. Hell, I'm pretty sure Lexie checked out my pupils. I'm good. Love you."

"Love you, too. Call me if you start throwin' up or get sicker or anything, okay? We've got your game–"

"I know, I know. Bye, Mom."

"Bye, baby. See you when you get home."

I click the phone off and shove it in my pocket. Jeez.

"Are you fine?" Cody's hands are wiggly, rubbing his knuckles. He does this when he's nervous.

Why is he nervous? He doesn't get nervous much.

The shift in energy is hard to know what to do with. How am I supposed to respond to him? He didn't mean to hit me. I know that. He didn't mean to take the girl I wanna be with. I never told him I like her.

My own fault on that one. I tell him most things. If I could turn back time, I would've long before he asked her out.

There's no way to change it.

I need to be happy for them. There's plenty of other people I can be with. It doesn't have to be Lexie.

My heart tightens up thinking about that. I know it's crazy, but I sometimes feel like she's my soulmate. I thought that about someone else before. But even that was different.

I don't believe in stuff like this, normally. Yet here I am, a mess of emotion that Cody's dating her.

He's still looking at me when I come out of my deep thoughts.

"I don't know. Okay, I just don't know." I hang my head onto my palms. Elbows over knees. Pressure on my temples. Wishing the throbbing pain would subside. Why does this have to be so complicated?

"I'm sorry." Cody's hand is on my shoulder. "I need to get a hold on life."

"I just don't get it. Why don't you want me to get lost so you can be with your girlfriend? On prom night? Aren't you supposed to spend the night with just her?" I look at the lake behind Lexie's house.

"I can't handle knowin' you're mad at me."

"I'm not mad at you." I focus on his face. The way he raises one eyebrow like he knows I'm holding back. It felt like a lie coming out of my lips. A lie that only he would catch.

"Maybe I am." I clear my throat. He gets the truth, even when it's hard to say it.

"I wanna fix it." He grips my shoulder tighter.

"Is that even possible?" I search his eyes, the eyes of someone who knows me better than I know myself. The eyes of the person who has shared most of my life with me. Especially my secrets.

"Look, this isn't what I want. Okay?" He looks at me for a long time.

"It isn't what I want either." I gaze into the kitchen where Lexie's sitting alone. She's got a chicken wing in her hand. There's barbecue sauce all over her mouth. She flicks her tongue out to lick it off, missing most of it.

It's freaking adorable.

She doesn't need our drama. I know she's trying to make the most of prom night. Wish I didn't have a headache.

"So Uncle Denver was supposed to give me forty bucks. My cousin's still in the hospital. Kevin's who knows where. He bought a bunch of stuff with my money and just like that the account's overdrawn. I did all this stuff for Denver. Alone. All day long." Cody's told me all about the junkyard. This isn't new. Every month there's something. An odd job he's done.

"And you didn't call me to come help because?" I tilt my chin down, stretching out my neck.

"It's my fly in the ointment, not yours."

"Doesn't mean you have to bear it alone." I reach under the Care Bears shirt for my cross necklace, holding it out to him. "Just as I have loved you,"

"So also must you love one another." We quote together.

"John 13:34. It's a classic." Cody runs his fingers along the baseball seam on the cross. "I love that you wear this all the time."

"You told me to." I tuck it back under the shirt.

"It suits you." He smiles.

"So what happened with the forty?" I have cash in my wallet.

"Butthole Denver didn't have it." Someone's always selling him short.

"He does this a lot. Take advantage of your work." I shake my head, annoyed that this is his normal life.

"Yeah, the power company is shutting it off Monday."

"Well that's good timing. We get paid on Monday. They'll probably let you bring it down late if you call." In February, I had driven him to Publix to pick up our paycheck. Took him to the power company. He argued with them for an hour to turn the power back on if he paid half the bill.

"I'll drive you after school. Anywhere you need to go." I hold those blue eyes of his until he agrees with a nod.

"I'm about to do something and you're not allowed to fight me on it. I'm done with that. We've fought enough." I pull forty bucks out of my wallet and put it in his hand.

The look on his face is a mix of shock and grief. Before long, he stuffs the money in his pocket. Good. I don't need it as much as he does.

We sit in silence as time stretches into eternity.

"Bobby?"

"Yeah?"

"This doesn't make what I did okay, and I know that." The sincerity in his tone reaches me. I guess this is how we've stayed friends. What's friendship if there aren't some ups and downs?

"You need to drop it. I'm tryin' to forgive you." I let out a long sigh, watching the waves across the water.

"I know you are. But Bobby, we can't move on yet."

I'm not sure we ever can, Cody. Not after everything else.

There's a pain in my chest that never goes away. I've had so much pain because of his choices. He's done so much to hurt me. I know he doesn't mean to. But he still does. It still hurts.

"I just wanted to tell you about the pressure and stuff. It's not an excuse. There's no excuse for what I did. And I wanna stop being a prick. I wanna be a better friend. Oh, shoot, I almost forgot I'm holding these." He opens his hand and there's two Tylenol. "Lex says you can have ibuprofen in a couple hours. She knows about all the doses and stuff. Well, I guess you probably do too, what with your dad and all."

I stare at the white pills. He bends over the side of the chair and gets a cup of water. Didn't even see him bring it out when I was on the phone with Mom.

"Thanks."

"It's alright if you're not feelin' good and wanna go home. But if you start feelin' better, we can all hang out. Like old times. It's been too long."

"It really has." I pop the pills in my mouth and drink the whole glass of water. I stand and offer him a hand up. "Let's hang out with Lex."

Cody

"Thanks again, Lex. You're a lifesaver." Bobby says as we pull into the hotel parking lot to get his truck. "It was fun to hang out."

"Sorry it didn't help with your mom." Lex parks the car and I get out to talk to Bobby. Can't stop thinking about today. Bout my stupid uncle. About how fucked up it is that I was so late that my best friend had to take *my* place and dance with my girl *and* that I hit him for it.

Like my mind can't let it go.

Of course I can't.

Not after all I've already done.

I'm so scared of losing him. The whole time at Lexie's house I just loved being with him. We used to have so much fun all the time.

I've changed and it's not fair to those around me. These are the kind of friends everyone dreams of having. We won the high school lottery because it's not just popularity, these are good people that I need to take care of. I have to do better.

My life may be shit, but it never means I get to take that out on them. All they ever do is try to help.

"Oh, it'll be fine." Bobby gets out of the car. His shirt went through three rounds in Lexie's washing machine. Looks good as new.

"Can't even tell." I run my hand on his chest, where the stubborn blood stains were.

"Lex is awesome." Bobby's voice still sounds sad. Or maybe I'm making that up because I'm still sad. I'm sad that I hurt my best friend. Part of me is even more sad that he sat here and took it.

"Ain't she?" I clear my throat, all kinds of clogged with this bullshit I've caused. Tonight was supposed to be special. And the only person I can blame for the whole thing is me.

"I'm glad you stayed." I search Bobby's eyes, standing outside, knowing Lexie's probably wondering why I'm taking forever to talk to him alone. With my peripheral I see that she's just scrolling her phone. We have time. All the time we need.

"I'm glad I did too." Bobby licks over his teeth.

"Look, don't go. Not yet." I find his eyes while his hand drops down to his hip. Taking a step closer, I smell his cologne, through the haze of Lexie's wash. "I'm not gonna be able to let this go." I hold his gaze, seeing the sympathy for me that he shouldn't have, but does. "I need your forgiveness, more than I need hers." My words hang in the air for a long while.

"You already have it." He's talking softly. "Please, just let me go home. It's getting late and we've got an early mornin'. Go have fun with Lex. Give her a good night. Show up for her."

Pain radiates through my chest. I've fucked up. And I want him to punish me for it. I want him to rage and yell and even beat me up. I deserve that. I don't deserve his grace. Or his money.

If there's anyone who should hate me and tell me to go to hell, it's him.

But he doesn't. He gives me a kind smile and forgiveness I haven't earned.

"See ya tomorrow," he gets in his truck. "Tell Lex goodnight."

I stand on the asphalt, watching the exhaust from his truck as he drives away.

"You alright?" Lexie asks as I buckle the seatbelt.

"No." I lean my head on her dash, wondering when I lost control. The evening replays in my mind. Over and over and over and over. Endless round of torment. Torturing myself. Need to go confess. Need to pray harder. Need to be better.

Better, stronger, faster, more.

There was that moment when I saw him with her. I lost it then. Control was gone.

What if I do that to Lexie?

I can't be trusted.

That pain in my chest gets bigger. "I'm terrified that I really am some monster. I was to Bobby tonight."

"No," Lexie puts her hand on my shoulder. "You're a jealous asshole, but you're no monster." She waits until I look at her. "Bobby and I were just dancing as friends. You know that?"

"Are you sure?" I turn, holding her hand. Why don't I trust her? Why don't I trust him?

"There's nothin' between me and Bobby." She laughs. "He likes to go out with all kinds of people, but not me. He wouldn't do that to you even if he wanted to." Her words make me feel worse. Why didn't I believe that?

Because I'm so scared of losing her that I risked losing him.

"Why wouldn't it have been innocent? Have we ever given you any reason to believe otherwise?" She gives me an incredulous look. They haven't. He doesn't. He's never made a move on her. Apparently when I lost control, I lost all trace of reason.

This cannot happen again.

"I'm all yours, baby." She licks her lips, bringing them to mine. "How about I bring you back to my house and show you? We can have a nice night together, I can take you to the game in the mornin'."

There's a glisten in her eyes that makes me want to give her more than I can.

"I don't know babe. Yeah, I was teasing you for yawning earlier but in all honesty, I'm exhausted." I think about telling her that I'm no good and she needs to break up with me. I think about telling her that this is all wrong. I think about telling her *why*.

"You just wanna go home?" Her expression kills me. I know her. She wants to fool around after prom. Of course she does. I'm her boyfriend. Why wouldn't we?

"Nope," I rub her hand. "I wanna be with you. It was sweet you took us to your house and got pizza and fixed Bobby's shirt and, and, everything. You're great Lex. I wanna give you what you need."

Even though I can't. I'll try. All I can do is try and pray harder.

The way she's looking at me says that she needs *me* tonight. That everything else is gonna have to wait. I think the last time we even made out before tonight was weeks ago. When was our last date? I haven't been taking care of her. Hell, I'm barely passing my classes since I've missed so many days of school. Don't get to see her in class if I don't show.

If I don't step it up soon, she may make that little moment with Bobby more than friends.

He's a better man than I am.

Maybe she should.

Lexie

I don't know how this is gonna go, but I see that Cody is too low to be alone. He gets in this place sometimes. I am an outsider watching.

Will I ever be more than an outsider?

"Let's go get you somethin' to sleep in, and your baseball gear for tomorrow." I drive toward his place. "You can check in with the girls."

He leans his head on my shoulder. "That'd be good."

"When does Kevin get back?"

He's been real specific about me not calling his old man any term similar to father. For how religious he is, I'm surprised he doesn't show more respect for his dad. But if he won't even tell me about what happened today, I have no hope for figuring out the real history with him, and *Kevin.*

"Not sure," he snuggles into my shoulder more. "I *am* sorry Lexie. I should be better for you."

"Know what my granna always says?"

"What?"

"The past ain't gonna change. But if you try just right, the future can." I let my head rest on his at the stoplight. Something about this is perfect. It's us. Together. For the first time in a long time. "I've missed you."

"I know," he lets out a heavy sigh. "I've gotta figure some stuff out."

"You gonna let me help?" I keep trying, keep hoping. What else can I do?

"Nope. There's good times comin'." He's always saying that.

"Maybe I can be the one to bring those good times." I rub my nose against his.

"One day soon, I'll be bringing them for both of us. That's a promise." His kiss makes me so dizzy I forget where I am.

This is how I know we'll be okay. I feel so connected to him, so much love that I've never felt comes from his heart to mine. That even on a really rough night that was supposed to be spectacular, he's doing his best.

* * *

WE WALK IN HIS FRONT DOOR, THE TRAILER'S A MESS. THE DOGS RUSH us and I kneel down to pet them in the dark.

He flicks the lightswitch but nothing happens.

"No." He flickers it on and off, on and off.

"The lightbulbs out?" I grab my phone and summon the flashlight.

"It's not the lightbulbs." He bangs the wall above the lightswitch. "They weren't supposed to turn it off until Monday." He stumbles around the junk on the old carpet, down the halls. "Mama? Girls? Girls?" He opens up the doors to the two bedrooms. "Girls!"

They don't answer. Must not be here. Frantically, he goes to the fridge and pulls out all the food. He dumps out a box and puts the mostly empty contents into the cardboard.

"Cody?" I put my hand on his shoulder.

"It's all my fault. All my fault." He shouts into the empty fridge.

"Cody, shh, it's gonna be okay."

"Can I use your phone?" He takes it out of my hands and dials his sister, Anna Mae. "Ma's workin' late? You took the girls to Aunt Josie's house? You have Toby?...okay, okay...yeah I'll call Willardson Electric tomorrow."

He throws a box onto the kitchen table while I light the way. "I thought they could sleep here tonight. I wanted them to be able to stay at their own house. They don't like Aunt's Josie's house. But they get so scared in the dark. They aren't comfortable without the air running. They're supposed to be able to sleep in their own bed. Why can't I give them what they need?"

He sinks to the ground and holds his head in his hands. It's more like he's talking to himself than to me, but I'm here. Always here.

I join him on the floor. "A problem with the power company?"

"All of this is my fault. If I was better. If I coulda just gone to the power company today. If I coulda made sure they were gonna be okay. I can't believe they shut it off so late! I rode my bike here before prom and...why would they come out so late to turn it off? We were supposed to be okay until Monday! Bobby's driving me over there after we get our paychecks! I cannot believe I let this happen! Again! I promised Anna Mae I wouldn't let it happen again! If Kevin would stop emptying my bank account. I need to change the account number. I need to get the money back somehow. Need to give the girls somewhere to call home. This is all my fault." He wallows in this unrealistic level of responsibility. I didn't know his dad was cleaning out his account. That's just so wrong.

"This isn't your fault." I put my arm around his shoulders.

He's cursing under his breath. Punching the linoleum.

"Cody, this isn't you. I promise it isn't you. Let me help." I tilt his chin up so he can look in my eyes. "Get your stuff. We can put the food in my fridge. Maybe we can get the power back on by tomorrow."

"I don't want help." He growls against his knuckles, infuriated with his situation.

"I know you don't. But you need it."

"You shouldn't have to do this. Go be with Bobby. He's better. It's all better at his house. Just break up with me. Go be with him. That's what you both want. I could see it with how you were dancing out there. He's the one you need. I'm just a waste of time. A stupid, stupid waste of time."

Feels like I got punched in the stomach. My insides hurt. He doesn't mean it. I have to convince myself he doesn't mean it. My eyes get wet listening to all this. I feel so much. No, he doesn't mean it. We're having an off moment. It'll shift. It's gonna shift. It has to.

Stay strong, Lexie.

But I shouldn't have to stay strong.

"Get your stuff. Let's go." I get up and pull his hands.

We drive to my house in silence. I go to the garage and make space for his food in our spare fridge. He hasn't said a word since we left his place.

I get him up to my room and we get in the shower. I purr against his skin in the hot water. He's in another world.

I'm the outsider, always the outsider.

"Let me in." I hold his gaze.

"I'm not good enough for you." He looks away.

"You don't even sound like yourself. We aren't gonna talk about this until you're feelin' better. It's not the time." I pull back, finish washing off and go for my jammies.

He lays beside me in bed, writing all his thoughts in his notebook-journal.

"It's gonna be okay." I whisper against his chest. When he finishes writing, we get comfy in bed. His skin feels natural against mine. That even though we've had a horrible and stressful night, he's my comfort. I feel safe with him again. He needs to find a better way to cope with everything. If I was going through all this, I'd need all the support I could get.

We look at the ceiling, the gentle hum of our breath against the dark night echos between us.

"I'm glad you're here," he puts his hands on mine. "I know that I haven't told you enough lately." He comes on top of me, kissing my lips. "And I want to. Because you need to know how incredible you are. How much you mean to me." He runs his hand across my forehead. "I don't know how you stay with me. I don't know how it is that you can be with someone who is so difficult to love."

"You're not difficult to love." I hold his eyes, knowing he doesn't believe me. He's the easiest person in my life to love. Everything about the time we share together is.

"I'm gonna do better." He scratches my scalp. I grip up his shoulders, placing kisses on his lips.

"I'm gonna be the one you deserve. The one you need." And he's back, the Cody I've come to love. Even though he's always dealing with lots of things people shouldn't go through, he's fiercely determined to be the best he can be.

"I'm excited to watch you play tomorrow."

"I'm gonna be lost out on that field." He collapses on top of me, the physical and emotional weight pressing me into the mattress.

"No, you won't." I pull him close to me, clinging for dear life. "This isn't your fault. If you don't have power tomorrow, let's get the girls. They can sleep over."

"I'll find a way. Can you drive me to Willardson Electric?"

"Of course. We'll go after the game."

"Okay." He runs his hands through his hair. "And Lex?"

"What?"

"Thanks for being here. You're the best thing in my life."

"You're the best thing in mine." I relax, waiting until his breath quiets and I know he's finding the sleep we desperately need. Holding him tighter I know he's where I belong. We'll figure this out. We have to. I don't see any other choice.

Bobby

Well, that was a lot.

I park my truck in the third garage port, and just breathe. My head presses against the steering wheel because it feels too heavy to hold up. All of this is so freaking heavy.

What a night.

Dad's car isn't here. Can't believe Mom wanted to call him out of work. Over reaction, much?

Breath heavy in my lungs, I go through the door and kick my shoes off.

Mom's waiting when I walk into the kitchen. "Oh, honey." She pulls me into a huge hug. I didn't know how bad I needed it.

"I'm here, baby. I'm here." Her hands rub my shoulders and I'm turning to her comfort like a lost child. Maybe that's all I am.

She pulls back enough to look at the marks on my face. A gasp comes out of her mouth as she gently touches around my nose. "Oh, baby."

I wince. She goes straight to the fridge for an ice pack while I plop into a chair at the table.

"Goodness, Bobby." She sits beside me holding the ice to my face.

"I took some Tylenol a couple hours ago." I hold the ice so she can move her hand away.

"You didn't throw up or anythin', right?" She's really worried about this. Probably from the time I got a concussion a few years ago. Makes her on high alert whenever I get a head injury.

"No, Mom. It looks worse than it is."

Dad walks through the door. "Doin' alright, Son? Mom texted me about what happened."

"I'm okay." I lean my head on the table, overwhelmed by how much they care. The pain in my stomach gets bigger the longer we sit. My parents aren't going anywhere. They're legitimately worried. It makes it all hit harder like so many moments tonight already have. Feels like someone's swinging a baseball bat at my stomach over and over until I'm just a heap of emotional bruises.

As the ice pack thaws, I lift my head up.

"You wanna talk?" Mom's face is caring. I could tell them every-thing. Even the things I vowed to Cody I'd never share. No, no, they don't need to carry all that. The burden is heavy enough on my shoul-ders since I took it off of Cody's as much as I could. As much as he'd let me. I wouldn't change it either. This is the life I'm meant to live, I guess. Taking care of my friend since no one else in the world does.

"Not really." I swallow hard. My parents have always been super good at showing up for me. I can tell them about tonight, I know I can. Maybe it'd help to get some of this off my chest.

"Well, we're here if you change your mind." Dad puts his hands on my shoulder, a gentle squeeze like a hug. I stare at their wedding picture.

Will I ever have someone in my life like this? That perfect sorta love. The way I feel for Lexie.

I'll never dance with her again. Never kiss her again. *I promise you, Cody, I'll respect that she's your girl. I won't act on my feelings even if they keep getting stronger for the rest of my life.*

Mom gets out of her chair and comes back with pieces of wheat toast with peach jam for me and for Dad.

"Thanks, darlin'," he gives her a kiss. "Midnight snacktime at the Andersons. Forecast for tomorrow, gloomy skies and black eyes. Maybe we'll plan a menu around it. Put some Black Eyed Suzys in the crockpot while we're at the field."

I chuckle at Dad's silliness, but it comes out more sad than anything.

"Did I ever tell you about the time Tommy socked me in the gut?" Dad drums his knuckles on the solid oak table.

"About a dozen times." I take a bite of the toast, recalling the story of him and his best friend fighting over a girl. Guess history does repeat itself. Don't have to spell it out, Dad already knows that's the only thing we have to fight about.

"Here," Mom sets ibuprofen and a glass of milk in front of me. "Get you a full belly and a good night's rest so you can play tomorrow."

I swallow the food and pills, hoping I can keep them down with how much my stomach's turning.

Taking the steps slowly, I ascend the stairs. Anxiety riddles my veins as my body tries to come down from tonight. From the way it worried my parents. From the way I was hoping I could keep it to myself if only we could get the stain out of the shirt.

I throw my clothes in a heap on the ground. Stupid fucking shirt. Stupid fucking Cody. Stupid fucking prom night. I turn the water in the shower to hot, running it over my body, avoiding the tender skin on my face that stings whenever droplets splash on it.

A while later I'm in a t-shirt and shorts, gathering up the rented tux for Mom.

Damn, do I look awful. In front of my bathroom mirror, I take a photo and send the MMS to Sam.

Me: Rough night. Can you talk?

Sam: Fuck...

Me: I know.

A second later they call.

"You alright, mate?" Their thick Aussie accent comes through the line.

"Yeah, just stupid prom drama."

"Can't win 'em all, yeah?"

"Thought maybe you can tell me about your week? Get my mind off all this?" I plop on my bed, needing to melt into the sound of their voice. The way it soothes me over the miles that separate us. Sam's the only one who knows all my secrets.

"It was a good week. Baseball was good."

"Yeah, I saw that article about your team." I smile, glad for the distraction. We talk for a while longer until I'm relieved enough to go to bed.

"Thanks, ya know, for bein' there." I grip my pillow to my chest, holding the phone to my ear.

"I'm always here. You know that." They mean every word, I can tell by their tone. "Hope you can rest and play well tomorrow. I'm excited to see you next weekend."

"Me too. Night."

"Night." They click off the phone and I doze off, welcoming the relaxation I urgently need.

* * *

MOM WAKES ME UP EARLY WITH AN AWESOME BREAKFAST.

"Feelin' any better, honey?" She sits beside Dad at the table.

"Some." I lie. Still feel like death warmed over, but I know I need to play.

"Well Dad's gonna bring you by the urgent care just to make sure." She passes the carton of orange juice toward me.

"I don't need urgent care, Mom." I pour my glass half full.

"Told ya he's fine." Dad taps his fork in my direction.

"You're not gonna believe a famous heart surgeon's assessment?" I'm getting all worked up, more than ready to move away from last night. "Dad would know if I was fuckin' jacked up." I raise my hands up.

"Isn't irritability one of the concussion signs, Drew?" Mom looks at Dad for a good long while.

"It's also the sign of being an eighteen year old." He puts his hand on hers. "I know you're worried. He'll wear his helmet when he bats. It'll be okay." Dad brings her close. "Bobby told you Coach checked him out right after it happened. If there was something to worry about, we'd know."

Mom takes a long breath. "Okay."

* * *

I somehow manage to semi-focus at the game. My head's not feeling good, but I'm able to play.

"Bobby! Bobby! Hit them home!" Echoes from the stands. The smell of sand and hot dogs fills my nose. I spit sunflower shells near my feet.

"Highway to Hell" by AC/DC blares through the speakers. It's my song. I dance in my cleats to get the blood pumping before I run from the dugout with my bat in hand. Stretch my back. Get in position.

"Batting fifth, third baseman for the Willardson High Wildcats, number five, Bobby Anderson." The sports commentator announces.

"Bottom of the ninth. Bases loaded," the other commentator says. I don't need to know the odds, but we have an out. This is it. Close game. Still down by three.

"Think Anderson can deliver?" The first commentator asks.

"Oh, I've seen him do it before. Coach Wayne knows exactly what he's doing with the lineup to drive home their final victory before the playoffs. This may look like a lost game, folks. But you never know with the power drives of the Wildcats. Especially Anderson." The second commentator says.

I work to tune out the noise. Focus on the game. I do a couple practice swings with my bat. Cody's on first, smiling at me. I got this.

The fastball looks like it's gonna land a little too close to my hip for me to really hit it. I don't swing. Judged it wrong. Coulda hit that. Dammit.

"Strike One!"

Jeez, I'm not in the zone. Cannot strike out. Need a grand slam. Can handle a base hit. Want a double.

Get in the game. Get in the game. I turn behind me to see everybody. Mom and Dad on the front row of the bleachers. And Lexie. She's got pom poms in her hand, standing with Trish and cheering, "Bobby! Bobby! Hit them home! Bobby! Bobby! Hit them home!"

Love seeing her watching us so intently. She's dreaming of working with the sports medicine team when we get to college. Can't wait to see how much she thrives in that environment. She's got so much spirit already.

Not helping me focus. Jeez.

I take a deep breath. The pressure's enormous. Luckily, I thrive under this kind of pressure. I can do this.

Stretch my shoulders. Settle into my stance. Focus on the next fastball. I swing.

Chink.

Ball flies way out in the outfield. My cleats dash against the sand as I race to first. The other team's still fumbling in the field. Not a grandslam, but probably a double. Thank fuck.

They missed the catch and are working fast to recover. We keep going. Cody's on third. I'm on second. Mickey's home with our shortstop, Benny. Game's almost tied. If Cody and I can both get home, we'll win.

The next hitter, Don, strikes out. Damn...I thought he had it. We have one more out.

Come on, come on. I consider stealing third.

I look at Cody, and like he's reading my mind he knows. *Get ready, crowd, for the signature Anderson/Jones baseball move.*

We invented this.

Coach Wayne puts in our weakest hitter, Nathan. It's our clue to steal home. After two strikes, he manages a line drive.

I nod at Cody. He's going for it. We're gonna win this game. Despite everything, we're gonna win this game.

Cody runs home in record time. They've got the ball, trying to get it to first before Nathan does.

I steal home.

"Safe!"

Cody grabs me and we jump up and down. The game is won. We did it. Together.

Lexie

"You boys looked real good out there." I sip my strawberry milkshake, with extra whipped cream, sitting in the booth at Shakey's.

"Thank you." Bobby smiles. Cody's in the back with his mom. We have a few minutes just the two of us. Trish and Mickey are supposed to get here any minute.

"I'm sorry again for last night." Bobby's face still looks awful and I feel for the pain he's going through.

"Sorry for what?"

"I should've known that wasn't okay. I wanted to dance with you, wanted you to have a good prom." His cheeks get a little red. "But since it was behind his back it ended up causing a lot of drama."

"I had a really good time dancing with you." I bite the cherry and pull the stim out between my teeth. "Cody was a real mess last night after you left. He was telling me I should leave him for you."

"No," he shakes his head. "No, no, I didn't mean to even make it seem like that."

"I know. Bobby, you've never even flirted with me. Cody was off base." I turn the corner of my lips up. "It was sweet what you did, really. The whole thing. You dancin' with me. You taking the heat after his outburst. You still hanging out with us. Didn't have to do any of it."

"I love you guys." He drums his fingers on the red shimmery table top, giving me a timid shrug. "Honestly it felt good to hang out again. It's been a while. Glad we're here today."

"We love you too." I watch his face absorb the words, like maybe part of him wasn't sure. "All we've got is each other, right?" We all say this a bunch. It's funny that we ended up friends. The ones who don't have what we need without each other, somehow filling that void with one another.

"That was real smooth Bobby." Mickey slides in next to him on the bench.

"I've never seen anythin' so awesome." Trish scoots next to me. "Codester still with Mama?"

"Yep, did you order?" I hand her the menu.

"As if we need that." She stuffs it back behind the mini jukebox. "Ours is coming."

"I am taking Cody to Willardson Electric after this." I lick whipped cream off my lips.

"What?" Bobby's eyes come to mine, a face of shock all over him.

"Yeah, they turned his power off again." I shake my head. "That's part of why he was so upset. We went to get his gear for the game today and they'd turned it out. I told him we'd go down to the office and see if we can get it sorted out."

"They won't be there on the weekend." Mickey looks like he's dealt with this before. Hell, he probably has. The only time I've ever lost power was when we get a bad storm.

"Did you try texting Laura? Her mom works over there and sometimes they can get a technician out on the weekend if you ask real nice." Mickey rests his elbows on the table.

"Oh, good idea." I pull out my phone and text her.

Cody comes out with a tray full of burgers and fries, passing them around.

"You workin' here too now?" Trish dips her fry in ketchup.

"Yeah, it's my second job." Cody climbs around Trish to sit by me.

"More like tenth job. And you coulda asked me to move." Trish brushes off her lap where some dirt from his cleats got on her.

"Power went off? Thought you had 'til Monday?" Bobby stares at Cody almost like he's hurt that he didn't know.

"Yep." Cody looks at the wall behind Bobby, heaviness lacing his tone.

I look at the string of texts on my phone and feel happy when I see them come through.

"Mickey told me to text Laura. She says her mom can help. Look!" I show Cody the texts. Cody jerks his head toward me, giving a look of betrayal. His chest rises, holding his breath until he regains some level of composure. As much as I feel relief at this option, I regret the words.

"You guys." Cody stares at the ceiling. "I told you I didn't want help."

"It's fine." I bring him close for a kiss. He resists for a second and it hurts.

"When are you gonna let us help?" I whisper against his nose. "It doesn't mean you can't handle it. I've told you a thousand times."

"Lex, it's my business." He grinds his teeth together. After a few long breaths, he softens. "Thanks for trying." His lips take mine and I part my mouth, letting him taste the lingering milkshake from my tongue.

"Mmm, strawberry." Cody nods at Mickey, "Thanks."

"It's fucked up that they turned it off after dark. How were you supposed to plan on that?" Mickey eats a fry. "You know, we oughta file a complaint somewhere. That ain't right."

"I don't know. If I wasn't so past due it wouldn't have mattered." Cody leans his head on my shoulder.

"It's gonna be okay." I remind him, snuggling him close. After a while, he gets over the embarrassment and stress enough to eat.

"Did you and Jimmy have fun last night?" I ask Trish.

"Was alright." She dips her fries in my shake.

"Here, I'm done. Have the rest." I slip it over to her.

"Thanks, boo." She spoons out a sip from the bottom of the glass. "You boys kinda ruined the night. What happened to all of us dancing together? You promised." She glares at Cody.

"Well Cody and I danced in the parkin' lot." I shrug.

"The parking lot?" Trish gives him a face that says how cheesy she thinks this is. "Well you two got to dance. But what about the rest of us? Don't you even care about your friends anymore?" Her words sting a little too much because he's been gone. We always have each other. But lately it hasn't felt that way more often than not.

My chest tightens up with concern. If we're this busy now, what happens when we get to college? I know it's all gonna change. But what if it doesn't change for the better? I've been banking on this. Have to be able to have something to look forward to or I'm not gonna survive more fights with Mom.

I rub my sternum, thinking about how determined Cody always is to make things right.

When I look up, Bobby's staring at me.

"You okay?" He mouths and I nod subtly. It's hard that Cody was saying I needed to leave him for Bobby. I'd never dream of doing that. Bobby's great, but I'm already in the relationship of my dreams. Cody was talking crazy.

"I got an idea. Anybody got a quarter?" Cody messes with the little jukebox sitting on our table.

"Yep." Bobby hands him a handful of change. Cody puts on "Celebration" by Kool & The Gang.

"Come on, you guys," Cody stands on the booth and jumps over Trish, earning a horrified gasp from her. He takes my hand and starts us all up dancing in the middle of the restaurant.

"You're a dork." Mickey shakes his head.

"We're havin' prom right here and right now." He grabs Bobby and Mickey by the hand and pulls them into the walkway with us.

"They're gonna say it's a fire hazard." Mickey pouts.

"Quit being so paranoid." Trish tells Mickey. "They'd only say fire hazard if we were moving tables around."

"Just dance to this song. I'm sorry you guys. I ruined prom and I'm sorry." Cody brings me close to him, dancing us to the beat of the music. He twirls me around and my baseball cheerleader skirt flies in the air. All of us play along, dancing and singing to the music even though we look utterly ridiculous and everyone in the restaurant is ogling. We keep dancing until I worry I may throw up all my lunch. The rush is everything I was hoping for last night.

This is the place where we belong.

Together.

Cody

"You didn't have to give me your money." I swallow the lump in my throat knowing he's not gonna wanna take it back. Bobby's got the most generous heart there is. But I don't deserve it and I'm gonna make sure to handle this on my own.

We went to the bank after school and I opened a new account so Kevin won't be able to bounce checks for a bit. I'll keep a little bit in the other one so he doesn't notice. But I'll be able to keep the lights on and avoid another ordeal–I hope.

Gotta break this cycle of living paycheck to paycheck. Gotta break the cycle of abuse. Gotta break every stupid cycle I've inherited from that maniac.

Better, stronger, faster, more.

Bobby and I walk up to my house. I've got the box of fridge food that I've been keeping at Lexie's place. Power came back on Saturday afternoon, thanks to my friends.

"And you didn't have to bear this alone. I keep tellin' ya that." Bobby can say this again and again but I don't believe him. They don't need my problems.

We walk into the trailer. For a second I hold my breath, wondering if it's really fixed. Willardson Electric coulda changed their minds. Last week proved they'll turn it off whenever they please.

Cold air blast from the ceiling vent onto my face. Recognition calms my racing heart. The air conditioner's running. That means there's still power to the trailer. I take a breath of relief. My sisters and Toby can sleep comfortably tonight far away from Aunt Josie.

"Do you think your dad's comin' back?" Bobby opens up the fridge and helps me put the bottles in. Ketchup. Piggie Park barbecue sauce. Sweet Cubed pickles like Mama likes in her egg salad...when we have eggs.

"Oh, he will be. When he realizes I've opened a new bank account, he'll come sniffing around for it."

"Maybe just keep cash separate too? Ya know, just in case." Bobby hands me an almost empty jar of mayo.

"Yeah. Somethin'. It's almost worth him taking our funds. Don't have to deal with his moods." I seal my lips tight. That was way too much. Bobby's already asked a bunch of questions. I cannot handle him connecting the dots about what Kevin likes to do. If he hasn't already. That icky feeling takes up the bottom of my stomach. The part where I wonder if Bobby really does know. Does he just give me cash 'cause he feels sorry for me? I don't want him to know. If he hasn't already figured it out, it'll destroy him when he does.

They say abusers don't understand what they do, claiming that Jesus gave grace to those hung on the crosses beside him. That's twisted. I'm all for grace, but how can Kevin really not know? I don't buy it. Maybe those hanging by Jesus on the cross were innocent. But this abuser–and I imagine many more–know exactly what they do.

"Don't you miss him?" Bobby's questions radiate pain through me, like picking at an infected scab just makes it worse. I oughta miss my father. I oughta be begging for him to come back home. I oughta want his love, no matter how twisted it is.

The weak parts of me do. But I can't live in that mode. I've had to grow up way too fast to give in to the feelings of loss, knowing I've never really had a father in the first place.

"This sounds awful, but no. I honestly don't." And I feel lighter saying this. We'll leave it here before I end up saying way more than I should, but Bobby can know I don't miss him.

Bobby's eyes are sad, but understanding at the same time. We live a very different life, but sometimes I swear we share the same soul.

"Look, I know you don't like charity–"

"I don't." I pull out my wallet and give Bobby the forty I got from the ATM after we deposited our paychecks this afternoon.

He looks at the cash and then at the empty shelves, "Cody, if this is all that's in your fridge–"

"Please, don't." I hold the money in his hand to make sure he doesn't try to give it back. "Mama's figuring out a grocery list and we'll stock up again soon. I got it. Things are tough, but I got it. There's good times comin'." I hold his eyes but they look so down-hearted it eats away at my hungry stomach because it'd be so nice if we weren't spread this thin. Mama keeps applying for food stamps. But that's just it. Kevin makes *enough* that we don't qualify. We just never see any of it.

"We've got practice in half a' hour. Come on." Bobby drops the money thing and I go get my gear.

There's a comfortable silence as I relax in the front seat of his truck.

"How's Lex?" He keeps his eyes on the road as we head toward the field.

"Good."

"I didn't cause you too much drama there, did I?" His tone's so thoughtful.

"Nope. She told me you were just dancin' as friends. I shoulda let y'all tell me that before I went bananas." I stare at Bobby's bruises.

Gosh, I really ruined his face. If hitting him wasn't a crime enough, making his perfect skin look this mangled surely is.

"She was really sad she didn't know where you were. And I don't wanna put salt in your wound or anything, but standing her up at prom? Even though I get why, it's just, it hurt her." He looks into my eyes and I get it. This is one of those moments when he's trying to be supportive.

Why does everyone think this is what I wanted? I would've given anything not to be at Denver's when Lexie needed me.

But of course it's my fault.

I feel the anger rise. The anger at not being understood. About being blamed. About not being enough no matter how hard I try.

I always have to choose who to let down. I can never make everyone happy at once. It's too much. My jaw tightens and I want to scream.

Nope, don't be like Kevin. Can't be like Kevin.

"Maybe you can do something special for her. Get her some cheese sticks, oh and I know, take her on a romantic picnic at Elerish Mountains to eat them...or something fun with the cheese sticks. She loves those." Bobby's still offering suggestions. I grind my teeth together hard. He means well.

"That's a good idea." I watch the trees pass in the window, thinking it weird that Bobby knows what she likes. I guess he knows what I like too. There's always Pringles and M&Ms at his place. He's thoughtful and observant like that.

But only about me and Lex?

Something I should've realized a long time ago dawns on me. I feel ill. Woozy. Distracted. Like I wanna think about anything besides this but it's all I'm gonna be able to obsess about from now until the end of forever.

All at once my fears are realized. I know I'm actually right. My suspicions were real. Though to Lexie it was completely innocent what happened on the dance floor to Bobby it was not.

He likes her.

Gracious sakes alive, why didn't you tell me? I wanna yell that, but I'm worried about what he'll do if he knows I know.

Gosh darn it. He's completely into her. No wonder they danced.

I was right!

But it doesn't feel good to be right about this. I knew he may be jealous because he isn't in a relationship and I am. But man, connecting the dots in this moment. It hits harder than I'm ready for. We've been best friends forever. Tell each other stuff. But he didn't tell me he likes Lex. This just makes it that much more clear.

Sure, I don't tell him about my abusive father. But I tell him everything else. Heck, I tell him way more than I tell Lexie.

And he kept this one to himself?

Gah! Bobby! How the flipping heck have you stayed quiet about this?

She's my girl. He can't have her.

The world slows down. My pulse races like it can't go faster. I cannot get mad at him. Not after this weekend. But oh, I am. Bobby didn't bother to mention once that he's got a major crush on my girlfriend?

I can't lose her. I know I was talking nonsense on prom night. But I cannot lose her. Especially not to him.

I put the thought in her head.

He has all the desire.

They're gonna get together and it's gonna be all my fault.

"It always is..." Kevin's taunting voice sends pain down my back.

Muscles and bones remember.

Nope, nope, Bobby's not gonna steal her away. It's obvious he won't. If that's what he wanted, they'd already be together. Nope, he's probably just got a little crush on her or something?

My body gets hot all over. Why am I afraid to ask him more about this? Nothing is off limits in our relationship. We talk about everything and then some. But I'm keeping my mouth shut.

He literally just gave me an idea of how to reconcile things with Lex. If he wanted her, he wouldn't do that.

That's because Bobby knows how to be a friend. I oughta be a good friend back. That means I should be considerate of how he feels. That's more important than me being right or being possessive.

I've gotta fix this.

Now.

"Are you sad I'm going out with her?" My voice is shaking as I utter the words. I have to see what he thinks. *Open up to me, Bobby. Let me know what you need to say.*

Our whole lives, we've been there for each other. He's listened to everything I've needed to say. And everything I've needed to keep quiet about. But I feel everything unraveling, wondering what to do about this. He doesn't know how bad I need Lexie. Hell, every girl in school is crazy about him.

"What do you want me to say?" There's pain in his voice, clear as day. How did we get here? I think about the last few years. The way we spend time in our group.

"Are you happy? With her?" Hhis look lingers so long that the car behind us is honking for him to drive his car through the light that's been green for who knows how long.

He startles from the honk and heads through the light.

"So happy." I do my best to act naturally even though my insides are losing their shit.

"Then I'm glad you have that."

I watch his eyes. They're heavy with so much he won't say.

"I do miss us, though." His eyes are pleading and it hits harder than everything else. I'm always struggling to find time for everything. The little time I give to Lexie is still way more than Bobby gets.

"I've gotta find some more time to spend with you when we aren't at school or work or practice." It's a promise I'm going to keep. He deserves that much from me.

"At least we have that."

"Lexie doesn't replace you. No one ever can." I let the words hang in the air, watching the way his chest rises and falls like it's hard to breathe. "I know I haven't been there. I want to be. I mean, how've you been? How's school? How are your folks?"

"Small talk? Seriously?" He chuckles. "You've gotta do better than that." He shoves my shoulder and puts the truck in park at the field. I reach into the backseat for my cleats. Bending down, I lace them up.

"Hey guys,." Mickey waves as we head toward the gate.

"Did you hear from the Suncastle coaches yet?" Bobby asks.

"Yeah, how's all that?" I adjust my bag on my shoulder.

"Um, yeah." Mickey looks at the ground. Bobby and I both got scouted to Suncastle and got offered scholarships and more play time as freshman than any of the competition. They didn't say anything about Mickey.

"They'll have tryouts." Bobby puts his arm around Mickey. "We'll make sure you blow them away and get a spot on the team."

"Hope so." Mickey sounds worried.

"My dad's driving us down next weekend to look for apartments if you wanna come?" Bobby's just good. He's just good. All that I wish I was.

I need to be more like him. He's the one I need to exemplify. Be there for him. For Lex. Be there for Mickey and for Trish. I know she's been dealing with some heavy shit lately. Lex was worried about her. I need to be there for my friends.

I watch Bobby and Mickey go onto the field, wondering how I have friends like them.

I have to do better.

For Bobby.

I'll do it for him.

To find out more about Bobby, Lexie & Cody
...read A Game Like Ours.

ACKNOWLEDGMENTS

As always, it takes a team of people to really bring an idea to a full release. I am so thankful for the many supporters I have who help my stories shine even brighter.

Thank you to my real life romance novel co-character, Josh. You really give me so many cute moments to use as writing material. I'll always love that you stayed up until three am reading the draft of this story to make sure I had your feedback on time to keep up with my production schedule. You have such good opinions. I'm lucky to have you. Thank you for continuing to support me living my dreams.

Thank you Taylor (@25thavenuewest on instagram) for all the comments, hype and feedback and being my final set of eyes to catch the little things I missed. Thank you for brainstorming with me and for fan girling about so many of my Suncastle characters. I absolutely love that you're a message away when I'm excited about a clip I just wrote or need an honest opinion.

Thank you Aimee (@caffe.and.books on instagram) for being an early reader and giving me your thoughts. I love talking with you about my stories and characters. Your encouragement means so much!

Thank you, THANK YOU, thank youuuuuuu Deanna Young. You're so much more than an editor. I seriously feel like you understand me and my writing so well. All your comments help me make my writing better. I will forever be your student, constantly learning from the things you pick up on in my writing that need more attention. I so appreciate you continually working with me.

Thank you M.K. Depner! We've had so many writing sprints and I so appreciate going on this indie writing journey. So happy to have your support and opinions.

Thank you Katie Ferriello for being my writing buddy and giving me great feedback on bits and pieces of this story.

Thank you to my team, fellow writing friends that share in your newsletters and on your social platforms, my bookstagrammers, my book bloggers, my booktokkers, those who write reviews that make me cry…you make this all mean so much more. I so appreciate everyone who shares my work.

And thank YOU, for reading. I've always wanted to share my writing with the world. You give me a reason to.

THANK YOU FOR READING!

**Read more about Bobby, Lexie & Cody
in the full-length novel:
A Game Like Ours, on Amazon**

Cover: The Art of Liz, Ashley & Scott Knapp

ALSO BY MARISSA J. GRAMOLL

A Game Like Ours,

Book One of the Suncastle Knights

College Baseball Series.

COMING SOON:

A Risky Play,

Book Two of the Suncastle Knights

College Baseball Series.

FOUR YEARS LATER

AT SUNCASTLE COLLEGE

A GAME LIKE OURS

To the outside world, Bobby Anderson is an attractive, charismatic baseball star.

But inside, Bobby holds secrets—including his closeted sexuality—and each secret alone has the power to destroy his carefully-constructed life.

WHEN HIS BEST FRIEND CODY DIES, BOBBY IS THROWN INTO THE unwitting role of supporter for Cody's grieving fiancée, Lexie. The issue? Bobby has long-harbored feelings for her that he never allowed to surface.

TORN BETWEEN HIS GROWING ATTRACTION FOR LEXIE AND DEVOTION to his deceased friend, Bobby is forced to re-examine his life and concern about divulging his sexual identity. Another secret spoken by Cody during his final moments eats away at Bobby's conscience, driving the wedge of Cody's death deeper.

. . .

ONCE THESE SECRETS COME TO LIGHT, WILL LEXIE EVER BE ABLE TO forgive them? Can she accept Bobby for who he is? Will she ever want anything to do with him again?

CAN LOVE CONQUER A BROKEN PAST?
Buy this heartwarming read, today!

PURCHASE *A GAME LIKE OURS* ON AMAZON

A RISKY PLAY

Zac Williams' loves the attention of being a starting first baseman for the Suncastle Knights. Girls wear his number. Charm has earned him internet fame.

But Zac wishes he had the perfect, easy life everyone thinks he does. Instead, he's fighting an internal battle every day. Then Trish shows up. She's everything he didn't know he needed and makes the demons in his head quiet for a while.

They promise to keep it casual. No strings attached. No pressure. No plans for the future.

Only, there's so much between them that it's impossible to ignore.

Zac can't keep juggling his baseball career, his internet following, and a girl who takes so much effort to keep from slipping through his fingers.

When he's finally ready to make a risky play, and go all in, she's determined to walk away before she's trapped....

Will Zac convince her they are made for each other? Or will she leave everything behind before he has the chance?

PURCHASE A RISKY PLAY ON AMAZON

ABOUT THE AUTHOR

Marissa J. Gramoll

ENCHANTING SEDUCTIVE
REDEMPTIVE ROMANCE

Lover of stories since before she could walk, Marissa has always had a passion for creating characters and worlds. Learning to read was a challenge, so she learned words by writing them–taking her notebook everywhere and asking total strangers how to spell. Since then, a laptop has replaced her trusty notebook and her stories have evolved into novels.

Marissa lives with her husband, two children and an endless collection of David Bowie hats. She enjoys reading in the sunshine, with a big bottle of chocolate milk and music playing in the background.

She also LOVES hearing from fans and being tagged in posts about her books.